He Had Already Decided That She Wasn't At All Beautiful

Her face resembled that of a troublesome elf he had once seen pictured in a book of fairy tales. Her nose was tip-tilted and scattered with freckles, her mouth too childishly full, and those haunting eyes of hers nearly swallowed her face.

Casey, he thought musingly, testing the sound of her name in his mind. She was an absolute jinx to any man who came too close. But he found himself wanting her until his body throbbed. He was going to have his Casey, he determined, or die trying!

NICOLE MONET

is an inveterate writer of romances who lives in California with her husband and daughter and makes writing a full-time career. "I write," the author says, "because I am a voracious reader, and I feel that in some small way, I'm paying back all the pleasure I've received in my lifetime."

Dear Reader:

SILHOUETTE DESIRE is an exciting new line of contemporary romances from Silhouette Books. During the past year, many Silhouette readers have written in telling us what other types of stories they'd like to read from Silhouette, and we've kept these comments and suggestions in mind in developing SILHOUETTE DESIRE.

DESIREs feature all of the elements you like to see in a romance, plus a more sensual, provocative story. So if you want to experience all the excitement, passion and joy of falling in love, then SILHOUETTE DESIRE is for you.

Karen Solem
Editor-in-Chief
Silhouette Books

NICOLE MONET
Casey's Shadow

Silhouette Desire
Published by Silhouette Books New York
America's Publisher of Contemporary Romance

Silhouette Books by Nicole Monet

Love's Silver Web (DES #2)
Shadow of Betrayal (DES #39)
Passionate Silence (DES #62)
Love and Old Lace (DES #133)
Casey's Shadow (DES #177)

SILHOUETTE BOOKS, a Division of Simon & Schuster, Inc.
1230 Avenue of the Americas, New York, N.Y. 10020

Distributed by Pocket Books

ISBN: 0-671-47742-0

First Silhouette Books printing December, 1984

10 9 8 7 6 5 4 3 2 1

America's Publisher of Contemporary Romance

Printed in the U.S.A.

BC91

Casey's
Shadow

1

~~~~~~~~

The four-deck ocean-going cruise ship sloughed through the swells of the San Francisco Bay, its conical wheelhouse adding a touch of whimsy to the otherwise massive craft. Steadily, it made its way from a berth in Jack London Square and headed in the direction of the Oakland–San Francisco Bay Bridge.

Beneath the wheelhouse and directly in front of the bow lay a tiny galley, and it was here that Katherine Delaney enjoyed an unparalleled view of the passing scenery while she prepared food for the party her restaurant had been hired to cater. The area in which she worked couldn't have been more than six feet wide and four feet in length, but its large windows made up for the lack of space.

Besides, she'd rather be alone in these confining

quarters, she thought, than in the lounge serving hors d'oeuvres to the guests. They were business executives from a large textile firm in San Ramon, who had chartered the boat to welcome their company president from Los Angeles. Her mouth twisted cynically. They were probably more concerned with impressing the big man than with welcoming him. Unfortunately, she was all too familiar with the politicking that went on in the corporate world. The tension in the conversations going on outside the galley was evident to her practiced ear.

God, how she hated the falseness in the smiles and the calculating appraisal in the eyes of the men on board. They were corporate sharks, their usual three-piece suits replaced tonight by pullover sweaters and deck shoes. The few wives and girl friends who accompanied them weren't much better. She had once tried to belong to that elite group, she remembered bitterly. For Hugh she had tried, and had found herself as out of place as Alice in Wonderland bending to stare through the keyhole at a world in which she didn't belong.

For her there had existed no magic elixir to help diminish her stature; that task was accomplished easily enough by her husband and his associates. She just hadn't measured up to their sophisticated standards. She soon realized she was at best an inadequate hostess and at worst an embarrassment to the man she had married. The embarrassment had ended when he demanded a divorce.

To her surprise, the helpless sense of inadequacy

caused by his departure faded quickly. It was replaced by a feeling of competence and independence when she entered the world of the working single mother.

Her brow creased with worry when she thought of her son. Jonathan was a happy, well-adjusted child who was just beginning to realize that most of his friends had both a father and a mother. He had been only two and a half when Hugh left them, too young to understand the ramifications his father's defection would have on his own life. But lately he was beginning to question why his daddy never came to visit, and she couldn't find any answers to give him. She found herself making up excuses and watching sadly as, with four-year-old intelligence, he absorbed the evasiveness of her replies.

As the heat in the galley increased, she tiredly brushed a steam-dampened wisp of brown hair from her flushed cheek. Heavens, it's hot, she thought, focusing her attention on the misting windows that separated her from the blessedly cool air outside.

She had a sudden urge to be free of the hot, cramped galley, to be out on deck in the night air and salt spray. But then she remembered the piercing eyes of the man who had been watching her earlier in the evening. Recalling the reason she had chosen to isolate herself in the galley, she went back to work. Nonetheless, his image refused to be ousted from her mind, and she became furiously angry when she remembered the brief flair of physical attraction that had flashed between them.

She hated the uneasiness he'd made her feel, and had made no attempt to hide her resentment. Although those light blue eyes were full of amused interest, she had done her best to ignore him. But his intense gaze had followed every move she had made until her stomach had churned with nervousness. As she went through the motions of setting up the buffet, she found herself longing to strike the contemplative grin from his mouth.

There was no doubt he was a superb male specimen, with blond, wind-tossed hair and a hard, muscular body showed to advantage in a cable-knit sweater and snugly fitting jeans. She was equally certain he was aware of his own attractiveness to the opposite sex. It was there in his assured stance as he leaned against the wall, as well as in the bored cynicism that occasionally appeared on his strong-boned face. His features were saved from being too handsome by a nose that looked as though it had been broken at least once. There was obstinacy in the angle of his jaw, and an occasional glimpse of hard demand on his sensually full mouth.

He was the type of man she avoided like the plague, she thought, and she would continue to do so while there was breath left in her body. She had suffered years of subjugation to such a man before tasting freedom, and she was damned if she would ever again allow her spirit to be caged. Finally, acknowledging her own cowardice, she had escaped to the relative safety of the galley.

"Are those canapé trays ready yet, Casey?"

As the cheerful voice of Marilyn Vecchio, her friend and business partner, intruded on her unwelcome reveries, Casey turned with a smile of relief. "Hot right out of the oven, Marilyn."

Instead of pouncing on the foil-wrapped trays, Marilyn sidled over to the table fitted against the opposite wall, and sat on one of the two available chairs. As usual when her energy reserves needed recharging, she began to smooth her midnight black hair from her temples with nimble fingers. Not that a single strand ever straggled from the tight chignon she habitually wore, Casey thought in amusement. It wouldn't dare!

"Mmmm," Marilyn murmured, leaning back in the chair with closed eyes. "I should have stayed here in the kitchen. It is so warm and cozy and blissfully quiet."

"I'll have you know these elegant surroundings are called a galley," Casey corrected. "The captain nearly snapped my head off when I asked him for directions to the kitchen."

"Don't mention that man to me!" Marilyn exclaimed. "The nasty old geezer tried to pinch me as I was climbing the stairs to look at his wheelhouse," she snapped. "It's just too bad I speak Italian when I'm mad. Otherwise he wouldn't have looked so cheerful when he . . ."

Marilyn's frown increased in direct proportion to her friend's widening smile, and she wagged a finger in Casey's direction. "Don't you say a word," she breathed, a distinct threat in her flashing eyes. "At least I face the world of men head on, with my shoulders back; with dignity and courage. . . ."

Apparently Marilyn liked the image of herself as a shining example of feminine fortitude, and Casey hurriedly interrupted her before she had a chance to think up any more adjectives. "If your shoulders weren't back so far, you wouldn't find yourself in trouble so often," she retorted.

With visible satisfaction, Marilyn glanced down at her full-busted figure and smiled. "I get your message, my friend."

"You get the message, but with your usual obstinacy you never listen. Your sister was saying much the same thing to me yesterday, and by the time she finished I was wondering how I ever got involved with you two hot-tempered Italians."

"You're just naturally lucky, I guess!"

Marilyn chuckled, her face alight with its usual animation after her brief rest. "Anyway, Sharon has the manner of an old woman. I am the true Italian, with verve and zest for life, while she takes after our sensible German mama. If she had a husband and *bambinos* of her own to fuss over," she concluded on a grimmer note, "she wouldn't find so much time to hassle me."

Casey's sigh held exasperation. "So you keep saying, but someday your matchmaking's going to get you a bash on the head for your efforts."

"Speaking of heads, if you don't get out of here and take a break, yours is going to be aching. Come on, help me carry the food through to our ravening public, and then you can go topside for a while. You haven't stopped working since we came on board."

Casey needed no second urging. She helped Marilyn carry the heavy hors d'oeuvres trays through to the buffet set up in the midship lounge, and disappeared through a canvas slat that led to the catwalk. She stepped gingerly over coiled yellow ropes, and when she finally reached her destination she leaned against the rail with a sigh of relief. She tilted her head back and studied the moon as it bathed the dark waters below with spangles of silver. A fine, salty spray soothed the heat from her cheeks, and her nostrils dilated with pleasure as the sharp, tangy scent of the sea enveloped her.

"Are you a pocket Venus paying homage to the moon?" a deep voice drawled.

With a startled cry, Casey spun around. Her eyes were wide as she watched a shadow detach itself from the side of the bow. He halted directly in front of her tense figure, and she heard him utter a muffled gasp as he studied her face in the moonlight.

"Not a Venus," he muttered hoarsely. "You're a sea witch, with eyes so green a man could drown in them!"

Three days later, Casey stood swaying, not on the deck of a cruise ship, but on a stool that wobbled precariously with every move she made. She was trying to clean her dining room chandelier and she groaned as her shoulder muscles protested the abuse meted out to them, then sighed tiredly. Stepping down from the stool, she looked at the heavy dining-room table she had pushed against the wall and decided a much-needed break was called for. After a cup of coffee she would be in better condition to raise the chandelier back into position, she thought optimistically. She ignored a suspiciously throbbing crick in her upper back, which didn't bode well for her overly large chiropractor's bill.

She shrugged her shoulders and winced, and the flicker of pain brought the aggravation she'd been feeling all morning to the surface. Damn Marilyn and her matchmaking! Through the galley windows, she had spotted Casey cornered by an interesting-looking male, and had hurried out to satisfy her curiosity before Casey found an opportunity to escape. It was Marilyn who introduced Casey to Chad Walker, none other than Mr. Golden Boy himself, the president of Walker Textiles. During the course of their conversation, he'd admitted to being unfamiliar with the Pleasanton Valley area, and asked if either of them could recommend a place to rent. Marilyn glanced surreptitiously from Casey, who was staring at her with a warning gleam in her eyes, to Chad, who was staring at Casey. With gleeful eagerness, Marilyn told him about the empty condominium next door to her friend's.

"Who should I contact about viewing it?" he asked, still looking at Casey.

Before she could lie and say the house was

rented, Marilyn blurted, "Oh, just call the manager of the Fairview Condominiums, he's the one authorized to interview potential renters. The Carstairs, Casey's landlords, own her unit as well as the one that adjoins it. But he's a Navy man, and has been stationed in Guam for a year. Casey promised to show the place for them and keep an eye on things while it's empty."

Casey wanted to push Marilyn overboard, but the damage was already done. She found herself agreeing to show Chad through the condo on Saturday afternoon with grudging civility, before she hurried off to the galley to seek an outlet for her anger.

Now Saturday had arrived, and Casey was thoroughly annoyed that her day off was going to be disrupted. As soon as she got rid of Mr. Walker she would forget her cleaning and take Jonathan to Santa Cruz, she decided suddenly. At the prospect of a few hours spent enjoying the summer-time delights of the beach and amusement park, she smiled. She didn't realize that her smile also held an element of relief at the necessity of cutting a certain visit short.

She was just reaching for the coffeepot when a knock sounded on her door. The staccato hammering made her start nervously, and as she went to answer it she wiped her damp palms on the legs of her jeans.

His grin, she admitted grudgingly, was as devastating as she remembered. Holding the door wide in silent invitation, she struggled to contain her irritation. She returned his smile with cool composure and said, "Good afternoon, Mr. Walker. If you'll wait just a moment I'll get the key."

"I'm not in any hurry, Mrs. Delaney," he said, and followed her into the living room.

The mockery in his voice was maddening, and she glared at him with resentment. "Well, I am, Mr. Walker. I'm planning a trip to the beach with my son."

He stopped abruptly and glanced at her in disbelief. "You don't look like my idea of anyone's mother."

He flushed when her eyebrows rose inquiringly, and as if to apologize for his bluntness, asked quickly, "How old is your baby?"

Past experience had shown Casey that most men were eager to enliven a lonely divorcée's existence until they learned that there was a child to be considered. Probably Chad Walker was no exception, she thought, hoping to discourage him with her answer. "Jonathan's four years old. That's hardly a baby in anyone's book!"

"No," he admitted softly, "but you must have been little more than a baby yourself when he was born."

Her reply was defensive. "I was nineteen."

His eyes swept over her sandals and lifted to leisurely explore her snug jeans and cap-sleeved T-shirt with tiny rosettes embroidered at the rounded neckline. "In that getup you don't look much more than eighteen right now."

She tilted her chin at a defiant angle. "Looks can be deceiving, Mr. Walker."

His teeth gleamed against his tan face. "I know," he admitted quietly. "That's why I'm here, to see if my imagination played me false the other night."

She shifted her feet, placing a little more distance between them. "I . . . what do you mean? I thought you came to see the condo."

He lifted a conciliatory hand, which he quickly returned to his side when he saw the warning expression on her face. "I did come to view the condo," he explained, "but I'll also admit to wanting to see you again."

"I can't imagine why," she snapped furiously. "You're an intelligent man, Mr. Walker. Surely you know when a woman's not interested."

"And don't you know a remark like that is more likely to spur a man's interest than his indifference, Casey?"

"I'd prefer Mrs. Delaney, if you don't mind!"

"Why, when Marilyn told me you're divorced?" His smile reappeared. "Casey suits you much better."

She couldn't seem to think of an appropriate rejoinder. Instead, with legs that felt as if she had cotton wool stuffed in their knee joints, she went to get the keys hanging on the wall beside the kitchen counter. When her elbow nearly knocked over the mug she'd earlier removed from the cupboard, she knew it was time to get a grip on herself.

As for Chad, he was happy to remain unobserved. He wouldn't have wanted her to see the silly smile that spread across his face at her stricken silence, any more than he wanted to acknowledge the reason for it himself. He was deep in thoughtful self-analysis when an angry cry sounded from upstairs.

There was one thing about Jonathan, Casey thought. When he yelled, he made sure the whole neighborhood could hear him. But there was an element of fright in his voice that immediately aroused her protective instincts. She hurried toward the stairs with a hastily muttered apology. She couldn't begin to understand why, but she was strangely comforted when Chad followed. She had treated him with unforgivable rudeness and she wouldn't have blamed him if he headed in the other direction. It was only what she deserved, she thought, flushing with shame at her lack of self-control.

They reached the landing, and with the ease of habit she skirted the toys scattered over the carpet, turning to issue a warning to Chad. He glanced up, but failed to see the tiny Matchbook car until it was too late. His foot connected, and Casey lunged at him as he began to fall. She reached out, but her groping hand merely succeeded in overbalancing him. In shocked horror she saw him catch at the banister railing, miss it, and fall backward. The back of his head hit the wall with a sickening thud.

"Oh, God! Are you all right?"

Groggily, Chad opened his eyes and attempted a

reassuring smile. "You'd think a grown man would know enough to watch where he's going!"

She blinked at him in surprise, her face softening into a tentative smile when he didn't show any anger. If Hugh had tripped over one of Jonathan's toys, she thought, he would have been furious. "I really am sorry, Chad."

"It was worth it to hear you say my name."

As he spoke he rose to his feet, and Casey steadied him with trembling hands. She was vividly aware of the strength of his arm under her fingers, the softness of his long-sleeved cambric shirt contrasting with the hard muscle beneath. Bewildered by the tingling sensation that shot through her at the contact, she let her hand linger just a second too long.

"Casey?"

"What?" she asked disjointedly, coming out of her reverie with difficulty.

"Your son's pounding on the door," he explained gently. "I think he's locked himself inside."

Obediently, Casey turned, finally hearing the sound of fists banging against the bathroom door. She hurried to the door and tried the handle, finding that it was indeed locked.

"Jonathan, you've got to undo the lock before Mommy can get inside."

"I c . . . can't, Mommy," he said, sobbing with both anger and fear.

"Why can't you?"

"Because it's s . . . stuck."

19

"Here, let me try, Casey."

She didn't react to the masculine hand that pushed her aside, except to send Chad a guilty look from beneath her lashes. "The lock's loose," she admitted. "I've been meaning to have it fixed, but I never got around to it."

"Just like a woman!"

Before she could bristle at the chauvinistic comment, he bent and began fiddling with the metal plate surrounding the doorknob. "Do you have a hairpin?"

Calmed by his air of competence, she nodded and ran into her bedroom. She could hear him talking to Jonathan while she searched her dressing table. The low rumble of his voice sounded as though it belonged in her small, two-bedroom condominium. I must be crazy, she decided, when she realized what she had been thinking.

"Here," she mumbled as she returned to Chad with the required object.

"Thanks."

She held her breath while he shoved the pin through the lock. It wasn't until the door opened that she expelled the air in her lungs in a sigh of relief. Jonathan ran past Chad and buried his head against her. She murmured a word of comfort in his ear before straightening to thank the man at her side for his assistance.

"If you have a hammer and nails," he said, "I'll tighten this panel for you. There doesn't seem to be anything wrong with the lock itself."

Jonathan, already recovered from his ordeal,

looked up shyly at the strange man who was smiling at his mother. "Can I help?"

He shifted his hopeful gaze to Casey. When he received no answer, he tugged at the bottom of her T-shirt until Casey's bemused perusal of Chad's features was distracted. "Jonathan, say thank you to Mr. Walker."

"Please, can't we go back to Chad?"

The beseeching tone of his voice was quite similar to that of Jonathan's, and she grinned while extending her hand in gratitude. "Then thank you, Chad."

"And may I call you Casey?" he asked, with a lift to his brow.

She nodded, and he asked, "Tell me, is that short for something?"

"Katherine."

His gaze lingered on her mouth as she spoke; his voice was husky as he asked, "How did you get Casey from a beautiful name like Katherine?"

The dimple beside her mouth caught his attention, and he only barely resisted the urge to press his finger against the tiny indentation. "I was christened Katherine Celia. It was much too ladylike a name for a tomboy, and my brothers started using my initials."

Realizing they were still holding hands, she hastily withdrew her fingers from his warm clasp. "And this is my son, Jonathan," she remarked with obvious pride.

Her pride frayed slightly around the edges when Jonathan asked, "Do you like my mommy?"

To Casey's surprise, far from being annoyed by the little boy's candor, Chad threw his head back and laughed heartily. Kneeling, he met Jonathan at eye level. "Why do you ask, Jon?"

"Because you look at my mommy kinda funny, the way my Uncle Bill looks at my Auntie Sally sometimes."

Chad struggled to keep a straight face. "What does Uncle Bill have to say about that?"

"Jonathan, why don't you pick up your toys?" Casey suggested in a strangled voice.

Except for a knowing look from Chad, her request was ignored. Jonathan slipped out of her arms and gave Chad his complete attention. "He says it means he's liking her a lot."

Chad nodded and ran his hand over the cap of brown curls Jonathan had inherited from his mother. "Then I suppose that funny look means I like your mommy a lot."

Jonathan wrinkled his nose. "Do you like little boys?"

"I like little boys very much," Chad admitted gently.

Jonathan looked uncertain for a moment before his grin appeared. "You do?"

Chad winked and then nodded. "Especially little boys who know their own minds. Think we can be friends, Jon?"

Casey held her breath, watching in awe as this man effortlessly charmed her usually shy son. She saw Chad's large hand reach forward and noticed with disbelief how swiftly Jonathan reacted. Before she realized what had happened, Chad was being led downstairs by Jonathan to search for a hammer and nails. She followed slowly, and listening to her son's unself-conscious chatter with a growing ache in her chest.

Armed with the necessary tools, the two males went back upstairs. The sound of pounding accompanied Casey's movements as she put on a fresh pot of coffee. She was pleased yet disturbed by Jonathan's eager acceptance of Chad's presence in their home. Although her son adored his "Uncle Bill," her neighbor and his wife Sally were more in the age bracket of grandparents. She sighed as she realized that, although she tried very hard to give Jonathan the security he needed, there was no way she could completely fill the void in his life left by his father's departure.

Hugh had never given his son a great deal of time or attention, but for a child of Jonathan's age his mere presence would be enough. If only Hugh visited the boy occasionally, she thought helplessly, things might be different. Frustrated anger twisted her insides as she considered her ex-husband's selfish disregard for his son. But her anger was quickly replaced with pity. Jonathan was a terrific kid, and someday Hugh was going to realize how much he had missed by not being around to watch him grow up.

The sound of Jonathan's laughter came from the stairs, and she quickly strove to disguise her mood. Chad seemed very perceptive, and she didn't want him to sense her tumultuous emotions. She could feel his presence in her home with every nerve ending in her body, and the sensation was disquieting. She would show him around next door, he would say good-bye, and that would be the end of it. The thought made her ache with a regret she wouldn't—couldn't—acknowledge.

2

Jon fixed the door for you, Casey."

She turned at the sound of Chad's voice and smiled at her son. "Chad said fixing things is another way for a man to show a woman he apprec . . . appresh . . ."

"Appreciates her," Chad said, grinning.

"Yeah," Jonathan agreed, reaching out to hug his mother. "I like you, Mommy . . . but Chad said I have to grow up before I look funny."

Casey laughed. Returning his hug, she said, "Thank you, darling. I like you, too."

Jonathan bent his head back against her encircling arm, and his face reflected his pride. "Chad showed me how to fix the lock, and I only hit my finger once."

Chad ruffled the boy's hair. "Yeah, but you hit

my thumb a couple of times. You must take after your mother!"

Jonathan giggled, and at the older man's suggestion, he left to replace the hammer and nails in the storage cabinet near the patio area. Casually, Chad lifted his eyes to Casey, and all amusement fled from his face. He saw her wounded expression and silently cursed himself for his careless remark.

"I didn't mean that the way it sounded."

She drew in a shaky breath and attempted a smile. "Yes, you did. But I can't blame you for thinking I'm a jinx after I practically pushed you down my stairs."

"You're uncomfortable around men, aren't you?" he guessed, while his glance traced the softly vulnerable curve of her mouth.

She tensed and then shrugged her shoulders. "Sometimes men make me nervous."

"I can understand that."

"You can?"

He took a step closer. Suddenly the warmth of his body enveloped her. The room started to tilt, and she found herself grateful for the hands that gripped her shoulders with gentle emphasis.

"It's your eyes, Casey. They glisten like emeralds and pierce a man with their fire. They're so clear and bright," he whispered, "and yet the shadows deep inside present their own challenge. Now you know why I, at least, can't seem to take my eyes off you."

He grinned as she hurriedly backed away, hot

color rising in her cheeks. "If I'd been watching where I was going the back of my head wouldn't feel as if I'd been hit with a ton of bricks."

"Then maybe you'd better let me take a look at it."

It was as good a way as any to distract him from the intimate direction their conversation had taken, and she used the opportunity to avoid the warmth in his gaze. "Sit down here," she ordered, approaching him in a no-nonsense manner and pulling forward a padded stool from beneath the breakfast counter.

"Yes, ma'am!"

Casey suspected his sudden docility was merely a pose, but nevertheless she was relieved. As he seated himself, she gratefully moved behind him. At least in this position he wouldn't be able to fix her with that compelling gaze. Emotions she never knew existed rocketed through her as she parted his hair, and she wanted nothing more at that moment than to be somewhere—anywhere—else.

"Chad, you're bleeding!"

With a distressed cry she hurried around the counter that divided her small kitchenette from the dining area, and searched in a drawer for a clean towel. As she dampened it with warm water her shoulders slumped in dejection. God! She was a walking menace to any male who came within two feet of her, she thought angrily.

It certainly wasn't because she was unused to being around men. Her mother had died when she was a baby, and Casey had been raised in a totally male environment. Her father and three older brothers had done their best, and as she trailed around after her siblings she had quite naturally evolved into a rough-and-tumble tomboy. She was quite happy in those days, she remembered, until the natural changes in her body began to mark her as unmistakably female.

Casey recalled with inward pain the lengthy rebellion she had waged against her own feminity. Her father and brothers had begun to lay down strict rules of behavior, and she had chafed under the restrictions they imposed. No longer was she allowed to be one of the boys. Instead, she became an outsider in her own home, and her brothers changed from companions to jailers. They interrogated her dates so thoroughly she didn't have to wonder why she was rarely asked out again.

Except for Hugh, she thought sadly. Her ex-husband had gone through high school with her eldest brother, Bob, and was a frequent visitor in their home. When he first asked her for a date, she was understandably eager. She liked him, and because her outings with Hugh had parental approval, she reveled in the unaccustomed freedom. Soon Hugh was her "steady," and as far as her family was concerned, their eventual marriage was a foregone conclusion.

"If that compress is for me, may I have it now?"

Chad was frowning, as though disturbed by her preoccupation. With a stammered apology, she collected the other items necessary for attending to his cut and placed them in front of him on the pale green Formica countertop. Hoping he wouldn't sense her nervousness, she again parted his hair with her fingertips. The golden strands felt thick and soft, and she held her breath as she gently explored his scalp.

"Chad?"

When she received no response, she cleared her throat and tried again. "Chad?"

His eyes were closed, his senses reacting pleasurably to the delicate scent of her flesh. "Hmmm?"

To his extreme regret she moved away, her eyes remorseful as she told him, "I think you're going to need stitches."

The sweetness of his smile nearly stopped her heart. "I don't mind, as long as you come along to hold my hand, sweet witch!"

Hospitals made Casey extremely nervous, especially hospital emergency rooms. She had been waiting for Chad to be seen by a doctor for the better part of two hours and she was beginning to feel the strain. The waiting room was filled with a wide assortment of patients in varied conditions; the screaming children were the most pitiable. The aroma of stale coffee and wet diapers mingled with that of antiseptic, and Casey found it difficult to control the lurching activity going on in her midsection.

Oh, Lord, she prayed, closing her eyes and

beginning to mentally recite the alphabet in an effort to distract herself. Don't let me be sick! Nervous tension always upset her stomach, but knowing the cause wouldn't necessarily avert disaster. She began breathing slowly, the letters of the alphabet giving way to numerical combinations as she valiantly fought against nausea.

Glancing surreptitiously at the man beside her, she forgot her own discomfort. If his tightly clenched teeth were any indication, she knew he must be suffering damnably. His eyes were closed against the glare of the fluorescent ceiling lights, and although he hadn't uttered one word of complaint, she knew his head must be giving him hell. Well, she thought, if it's true that misery loves company, we're one heck of a compatible pair. She sighed audibly.

"Are you worrying about Jonathan?" Chad asked, eyeing her uneasily.

She shook her head. "My neighbors, Sally and Bill, are more than capable of handling him, and Jonathan enjoys their company."

"They seemed a likable couple," he remarked, having met them when they dropped Jonathan off on the way to the hospital.

"They're darlings," she said, her eyes revealing her fondness for her friends. "I don't know how I would have managed when Hugh left if it hadn't been for them."

His body stiffened. "Your husband?"

She grimaced and looked down at her clasped

hands. "Sometimes I find myself wondering if he ever was. Poor Hugh! I just can't find it in my heart to blame him for finding our home life irksome. He wanted a poised, confident hostess with whom to impress his business acquaintances. I'm afraid I fell sadly short of the mark."

"Surely that isn't all the man required in his wife."

"No, but I wasn't much use to him in other areas, either," she admitted. "The president of Hugh's firm had a daughter who was fond of soothing my husband's fevered brow. I like to think she was something of a sophisticated masochist, but that's just my opinion. Anyway, Daddy-dear transferred Hugh to the Chicago office, and my spouse did what was expected of him. He filed for divorce and left all his problems behind when he moved."

"And he married Daddy-dear's offspring?"

He glanced at her in surprise when laughter bubbled from her throat. "No, and I suppose Hugh blames me for that, too. As far as I can deduce, his move to Chicago put him on top of the world. His life was on an upward swing, and I'm afraid he reacted accordingly. Miss Sympathy found a needier brow to soothe, and happy Hugh was left high and dry."

A muscle pulsed in his jaw. "Is there a chance of a reconciliation?"

"A year ago I might have been desperate enough to swallow my pride, but not any longer. I married Hugh when I was eighteen. We moved to San

Ramon because of his job. My family is still in southern California, so when he left I had to face the world on my own. That wasn't easy with only a high-school diploma and no experience."

"How did you manage?"

"I began working as a waitress, and I discovered quite a few things about myself. I love being with people, and I enjoy the feeling of satisfaction I get from making my own way. Regular customers began asking to be placed in my section," she said, smiling, "even the men whose soup I spilled in their laps."

She had to wait for his laughter to subside before continuing. "I became good friends with Marilyn, who helped train me. When she and her sister decided to open their own restaurant, they asked if I'd be interested in a three-way partnership. I had a little money left from the divorce settlement, and the risk only added to the excitement of owning my own business. It was rough going at first, but since we started catering things have been looking up."

"You're obviously a busy lady. Doesn't that make caring for Jonathan difficult?"

She looked wistful for a moment. "I can't spend as much time with him as I'd like, but with Sally's help we manage to get along fine. When I work mornings he attends a day nursery, and when I have to work evenings Sally picks him up and keeps him with her."

Amazed that she'd practically given Chad her life history, she stopped her chattering abruptly. She didn't know what had made her confide in him to such an extent. She wasn't usually so forward with strangers, especially men. Maybe it was his attitude of genuine concern that had bypassed her usual shyness, she thought, but she'd bent his ear long enough. She decided to sit as quietly as possible and lapsed into what she hoped was a dignified silence.

She wasn't successful, but the sound of Chad's voice brought a halt to her fidgeting. "You really are self-conscious around men, aren't you?"

At that moment the nurse called his name, and in her relief, Casey almost hugged the buxom woman. But her relief was short-lived when Chad got to his feet and pulled her up with him. Capturing her hand in his, he dragged her behind him while he followed the nurse down the corridor.

"I can't go in there with you," she hissed, trying to pry his fingers loose with her other hand.

"Why?" he questioned her teasingly. "They won't ask me to strip just to look at my head."

"That's not the point," she argued, with an unsuccessful jerk of her arm. "You're a big boy now, and fully capable of taking your medicine without my help."

"But I want you," he replied smoothly.

A shiver traced a path down her spine at the tone of his voice. She stumbled and would have fallen if he hadn't transferred his grip from her fingers to her waist. If she thought, in the brief instant that his hand released its hold, that her chances of escape were better, he soon disabused her of that notion. His arm clamped her to his side like a steel band and his eyes sparkled dangerously as she lifted her head to scold him.

"What will the doctor think?"

He shrugged his shoulders with complete unconcern. "Probably that you're my woman, not that it matters."

"Well, I'm not," she cried.

"Don't be so sure!"

Casey avoided the nurse's amused stare as Chad pulled her through the examining-room door. She broke away from him and stood rebelliously in front of a chair in the corner. "This tendency toward sarcasm is not a nice trait, Mr. Walker."

"I'm not trying to be nice, honey."

She crossed her arms over her chest. "Don't call me that!"

"Calm down, my sweet little witch."

"Don't call me that either," she hissed, her eyes sparkling threateningly. "I'm not your honey, or your witch. I'm not your anything!"

"Ah, but you're going to be."

She shook her head, and paused for emphasis between words. "We . . . are . . . nothing more than . . . strangers!"

"That's a mere technicality."

A heavy silence followed his assertion, and Chad used the opportunity to study Casey's mutinous features. He was fascinated by the conflicting emotions in her eyes. A surge of desire swept through him as he found himself wondering if the color in those emerald eyes would deepen when he made love to her. The erotic question barely registered in his mind before he knew the answer. Oh, yes, he thought, not in the least surprised when he felt himself shiver with unmistakable anticipation. In the short time he had known her he had seen her eyes show dismay, remorse, fear, gratitude, shyness, and uncertainty. They were like a barometer gauging her emotions, he realized. It would be up to him to make certain pleasure was added to the list.

He was in the process of mentally stripping Casey of her clothes when the doctor bustled into the small box of a room. While she introduced herself he glanced from her to Casey. He smiled his satisfaction.

Casey responded to his grin with a disgruntled sniff. To her chagrin, the attractive and rather voluptuous physician turned her elegantly coiffed head to look at her. One perfectly plucked eyebrow rose, and Casey noticed the amused quirk of the woman's lips with a twinge of anger. Straightening her spine, Casey began to tug self-consciously at her wrinkled T-shirt.

Chad began to describe his injury, and Casey scowled at him. The doctor chose that moment to glance at her again. Obviously deciding that Casey's frown reflected worry, she attempted to relieve the tension in the atmosphere by asking, "Is your husband usually this accident-prone, Mrs. Walker?"

Oh, Lord! She had tried to warn him, but would the stupid man listen? Oh, no! He had to drag her into this situation, placing her in an extremely embarrassing position. Well, she wouldn't give him the satisfaction of going along with this farce, she decided. She avoided the unholy amusement in Chad's eyes by tilting her chin pugnaciously in the doctor's direction.

"He's not!"

Casey flushed at the brusqueness of her statement and tried to rectify the situation. "I mean, he's not . . ."

Another voice interrupted. "My wife's trying to tell you I'm not at all accident-prone, doctor."

He sent a distinctly forbidding glance at Casey, then smiled at the doctor. "She's a little shy with strangers."

The doctor sent Casey an encouraging look. "We're all inflicted with shyness at one time or another, Mrs. Walker. I'll get to work, and you can take your husband home in short order."

Casey wasn't in the mood for encouragement. "You can keep him!"

The doctor looked extremely uncomfortable, shifting nervously from one foot to the other. "Um, yes. Well, I'll just get on with it, then."

Casey drew in a steadying breath. "I'm afraid he needs stitches."

She moved to stand beside the doctor while Chad shoved himself onto the examining table. When Casey approached, he casually ran his hand over her disordered curls before meeting the doctor's glance. "She's a little worrywart," he remarked fondly.

"Possibly," the doctor admitted with a relieved laugh, "but it doesn't do to ignore head injuries. I think it will save our patient a great deal of discomfort if you point out the exact position of the wound, Mrs. Walker."

The doctor was beautiful, intelligent, and enviably tall. As Casey looked up into her brown eyes, she wished she could find a single fault in the poised woman at her side. She found none.

With a peremptory motion Casey gestured to Chad, and he obediently altered his position on the table. The woman's hands reached out to gently part his bloodied hair, and Casey firmly suppressed a twinge of jealousy.

"Mmmm, rather nasty," the doctor murmured, "but since the bleeding's stopped I don't think it will require stitches. How did it happen?"

"Casey pushed me down the stairs," he replied cheerfully.

"You know I didn't mean to push you, Chad Walker!"

Casey squirmed when the doctor glanced at her with suspicion. "I see."

Chad laughed softly. "I wonder if you do."

She looked contemplatively in Casey's direction before returning her attention to Chad. "Would you like to explain further, Mr. Walker?"

"Not on your life, doctor."

By the time the emergency-room doors closed behind them, Casey was spoiling for a fight. When Chad, who was strolling at her side, began casually whistling an off-key tune between his teeth, her anger erupted. "How dare you tell that doctor I was your wife!"

"I wasn't up to long explanations."

"You could have just left me in the waiting room."

"I was afraid you'd make a run for it," he explained patiently, seating her in her car before moving around to the passenger side.

"I should think you'd be glad to get rid of me." She twisted the key in the ignition, raising her voice to be heard over the sound of the engine.

"I knew you'd get around to thinking that way sooner or later."

His tone was so smug that she retorted heatedly, "You don't have the intelligence of a flea!"

His voice sounded completely innocent when he said, "Don't you think so? Odd, I thought it was very smart of me to admit I shouldn't drive after being slammed into your wall."

His good humor was beginning to grate on her nerves. "I think that knock on the head made your brain fuzzy. If you knew what was good for you," she concluded morosely, "you'd jump out of this car at the next red light and start running."

He let out a bellow of laughter, nearly causing her to miss the turn onto her street. "You're priceless!"

"I'm dangerous," she snapped. "You're not the

only man I've injured with my clumsiness, you know."

"Lethal," he agreed, lowering his long legs to the ground as soon as the car rolled to a halt. It didn't take him long to reach her, and she was still smarting from his remark when he placed his hand beneath her elbow and hauled her onto the pavement.

"Doesn't that worry you?" she asked.

"Not a bit."

He considerately slowed to match her shorter stride as they circled the shrubbery lining the path. "Just where do you think you're going?"

"Into the house," he stated, a devastating smile crinkling the corners of his eyes before spreading to his mouth. "With you."

She whirled, her hands on her hips. "Look, I appreciated your help with Jonathan. I'm sorry your chivalry cost you a good deal of pain, but I've done my best to make amends. In fact, I think I'm actually the injured party here. You received a cut on the head that didn't, I might remind you, require stitches. But I've been harassed, humiliated, and suspected of being a husband-beater!"

Her indignation was met by a loud guffaw. "God, the look on her face was indescribable!"

Casey's lips twitched, but she maintained her sternest expression. "I fail to understand your perverted sense of humor!"

Another outburst of laughter followed the first, and he leaned weakly against the frame of her front door. "I haven't laughed this much in years," he gasped, completely unself-conscious about the tears trickling down his cheeks. He took a swipe at his face with the back of his hand.

Casey shoved her key in the lock. "You're giving me a headache."

He followed her through the door and closed it behind them. With all the panache of a man used to adapting to his surroundings, he lifted a battered teddy bear off the couch and usurped its position. His shoes thumped against the carpet and, with a loud sigh of satisfaction, he stretched out on the sofa.

"Just make yourself at home, why don't you?"

He opened his eyes, and focused sleepily on her. "Thank you, sweetheart."

She sighed with impatience. "Why don't you let me drive you to wherever it is you're staying? I suppose friends are putting you up temporarily?"

"No," he stated, and arranged his body more comfortably against the lumpy surface of her well-used couch. "I flew in from Los Angeles for the party and preferred to check into a motel." He grinned. "I like my privacy."

"Then there's no one to look after you?" she exclaimed worriedly.

"Nope." He shook his head, then winced. "Casey, do you have any aspirin?"

She was immediately contrite. Here she was, giving him the third degree and resenting him for making himself at home on her couch, when it was her fault he was laid up in the first place. With a

40

murmur of distress she hurried into the bathroom, and returned carrying two aspirin and a glass of water.

"Thank you," he said, raising himself on his elbow and accepting the aspirin. Popping both pills in his mouth, he drank thirstily. "I feel as though I've been run over by a semi."

Casey winced guiltily. "Would you like something to eat? It's nearly eight o'clock, and you must be starving."

"Do you want me to run next door and get Jon?"

"Sally has a steadfast rule," she replied. "If I'm home later than seven o'clock, she goes ahead and puts him to bed. She doesn't like the idea of his being shuttled from one bed to another after he's settled for the night."

Casey was tucking the ends of her T-shirt into her jeans, and so missed the anticipatory gleam in his eye. "Then if it's no trouble, I would enjoy sharing your dinner," he answered.

She was halfway to the kitchen when her brain registered the humble meekness of his reply, and she turned to glance at him suspiciously. He was lying quietly, his eyes closed once again. He looked endearingly pathetic with his hair rumpled and his stockinged feet draped over the end of the couch. But there was a suppressed vitality in his reclining figure that made her pause to wonder if he was quite as debilitated as his posture indicated. At that moment he uttered a tired groan, and Casey felt a surge of pity. Shrugging her shoulders, she turned her attention toward the contents of her refrigerator.

Chad crossed his arms behind his head and grinned his satisfaction, but he kept his eyes closed through necessity. A dull ache pounded inside his skull, but as far as he was concerned it was a small price to pay for bringing Casey into his life. And she *was* in his life, he thought. What surprised him wasn't the realization, but his own reaction to it. Where women were concerned, he was a short-distance sprinter. He hadn't wanted the complications of a lasting affair, and as a result he'd always gravitated toward women who were more interested in what he could give them than what he was as a person.

That Casey was different went without question. She was obviously proud of her independence. He visualized her and his pulse responded accordingly. She was just a little scrap of a thing, without any of the poise and artful femininity he had come to take for granted. He had already decided that she wasn't at all beautiful. Her face resembled that of a troublesome elf he had once seen pictured in a book of fairy tales. Her nose was tip-tilted and covered with freckles, her mouth too childishly full, and those haunting eyes of hers nearly swallowed her face.

As he lay listening to the object of his thoughts moving about in the kitchen, he was awed by the emotions her closeness stirred in him. Casey, he thought musingly, testing the sound of her name in his mind. Her head barely reached the middle of his chest, her breasts were tiny, and she was an absolute jinx to any man who came too close. But none of that mattered to him in the least, and he found himself wanting her until his body throbbed. He was going to have his Casey, he determined, or he was going to die trying!

3

By the time the hands of his watch pointed to nine-thirty, Chad was beginning to think it would be easier to slit his throat than to try to make any progress with Casey. To make matters worse, along with frustration, he was suffering from a mild case of indigestion. But that wasn't her fault, he admitted to himself.

She had fixed spaghetti, along with hot rolls and salad. Chad stared inattentively at the television screen, his mouth curved in a reminiscent smile. After he'd helped her secure the chandelier and move the table back into the center of the dining area, she had returned carrying the heaping platter of pasta. She was flushed from the heat of the kitchen, her hair curling against her cheeks in adorable little wisps.

"I hope you like spaghetti," she said.

She had looked so proud of her offering, he hadn't had the heart to tell her he had difficulty digesting tomatoes. In fact, after she had watched him lift the first bite to his mouth with an endearing air of anticipation, he quickly emptied his plate. He had even asked for seconds, he remembered, ruefully rubbing his hand against his stomach.

"Would you like a slice of apple pie?"

He jumped, and turned his head in her direction. The width of the couch separated them, and he found himself wondering how he could get closer to her without scaring her off. She had spent the time since dinner clearing the table, doing dishes, plumping pillows, and generally driving him crazy.

She had refused his offers of help, edged away from him whenever he got too close, and kept herself in a state of perpetual motion. She obviously thought that if she kept moving he wouldn't be able to make his move. When the silence between them had stretched to unbearable proportions, he had asked her permission to switch on the television. Her sigh of relief had been quite distinct, he remembered.

"Would you like some pie?" Casey repeated, reclaiming his attention.

He focused his eyes on her face, and immediately sensed an increase in her nervousness. She had been quiet for the last half hour or so, and he had begun to hope she was finally beginning to relax in his presence. But now she was shifting nervously along the edge of the couch, and he couldn't for the life of him figure out what had caused the change. He began to register the sound coming from the TV. Of course! The station was airing a commercial, and she needed to do something to fill the gap. God, was he ever slipping!

"I'd rather have a couple of Rolaids if you have them," he muttered, glaring at her accusingly.

Her eyes widened in alarm, and she jumped to her feet. "Are you drowsy?" she squeaked, kneeling by his side.

"I asked for Rolaids, not No-Doze," he retorted, still trying to come to grips with the certainty that sexually he left her cold.

The hand she placed against his forehead was not only cold, it was clammy. But as his gaze shifted to the pulse pounding frantically against her smooth white throat, he felt encouraged. Maybe his closeness didn't leave her unmoved after all, he thought in satisfaction.

"Do you feel like throwing up?"

He lowered the hand that had started to reach for her. "I beg your pardon?"

She bit her lip and rocked back on her heels. "You could be suffering from concussion," she exclaimed worriedly. "The doctor advised me to watch for signs of nausea or sleepiness."

Disgruntled at the idea of being mothered by her, he got to his feet and pulled her up beside him. "Since you seem to be preoccupied with throwing up, I think it's time I left."

She clutched at his arm. "You shouldn't be alone

after suffering a head injury, Chad. It's still early. Why don't you rest a little while longer?"

"Don't you have to work tomorrow?"

"No," she said, her expression pleading.

"I can't stay here all night," he argued, exasperated by her reason for wanting him to stay.

Her expression brightened considerably. "Why didn't I think of that?"

With a relieved smile she drew him back toward the couch. "I changed the sheets on Jonathan's bed just this morning. It's a junior and might be a little short for you, but it has a comfortable mattress," she babbled, some of the anxiety leaving her expression. "You'll be much better off here than alone in a motel, where no one would hear you if you called for help. You've had a very upsetting day and you shouldn't exert yourself unnecessarily."

If she had an inkling of the manner in which he wanted to exert himself, he thought, she'd be the one to shove him through the door, and she'd throw the dead bolt shut behind him. It was clear she felt responsible for his injury, but he was damned if he was going to give in to his desire to stay with her by feeding her guilt. It would be easy to take advantage of the situation—too easy. He was beginning to suspect she wasn't as indifferent to him as she made out. As for himself, he was having great difficulty preventing himself from pouncing on her. Just the thought of having her body beneath his on the rug made sweat bead his forehead.

"Oh, Lord, you're perspiring," she gasped, lifting her arms and wrapping them around his waist. "The doctor didn't mention perspiration. Do you think that's another sign?"

He closed his eyes, his body automatically swaying into hers. No more of a sign than rapid breathing, he thought, envisioning the way her naked breasts would feel pressed against his chest. Her arms tightened to support his weight, and he was suddenly afraid he was fighting a losing battle against his libido.

"I'm all right, Casey," he said through gritted teeth.

"You're not," she cried, holding on for all she was worth. "You're shaking like a leaf."

She tugged his shirt free of his pants and spread her hands against his back. "You must be running a fever, too. Your skin feels like a furnace."

He had tried valiantly, but at the touch of her hands against his flesh Chad knew that the battle was lost. Gone were his noble thoughts of protecting her from his lust. His brow furrowed with indecision. She was caring, gentle, obviously concerned for his welfare, and only a bastard would take advantage of her good nature. So . . . I'm a bastard, he thought. God! She had to know what she was doing to him. She was no naive little girl. She'd been married, and she'd had a child. No, Casey was no novice when it came to the intimacies of a man—woman relationship, so maybe she was playing a little game of her own.

The idea took root and served to lighten his conscience. Keeping his eyes closed, he spanned her waist with his hands and pressed his mouth against her temple. He would play the game to win, but he would play it clean. There would be no fouls and no unnecessary roughing. She would have no complaints, he promised himself, his pulse leaping as he inhaled the lemony fragrance of her hair. She would enjoy this as much as he would. He would see to that!

A moan escaped his lips; the warmth of his breath fanned her ear. He felt her shudder, the movement so sweetly evocative he had to clamp his teeth together tightly.

"Are you in a lot of pain, Chad?"

"Oh, God . . . yes," he hissed, burying his nose against the side of her neck.

"Where do you hurt?"

"All over." The mumbled reply was uttered with heartfelt sincerity, and he shivered as his thoughts centered in the area causing the deepest ache.

"Are you chilled?"

Are you kidding? he thought, taking note of the tiny, hardening buds that pressed against her knit T-shirt. I'm as hot as hellfire!

"Let me help you upstairs, Chad."

Pushing herself away from him, Casey turned off the television and the downstairs' lights, and checked the locks on both doors before returning to the living room. The only illumination guiding their steps as they climbed came from the upper landing, and Chad felt frustrated at his inability to read Casey's expression. He sensed a tension in her small frame that he was at a loss to understand. He decided it must be nervousness. He found himself wondering if he was the first man since her divorce to be invited into her bedroom. Glancing speculatively at her profile, he found the prospect elating.

"Wait here a moment."

Chad halted in the middle of the hallway. Before he had a chance to follow her Casey had returned, and his face showed his bewilderment as he saw the lightweight cotton robe thrown over her arm.

"This is one of those kimono-type wraparounds," she explained, crossing the hall as she spoke. "It's supposed to fit all sizes, so you should be able to wear it instead of pajamas."

She led him through a doorway across from her own bedroom. She switched on the light as she passed it, and folded the robe carefully across the foot of the single bed in the corner. "I . . . I'm sorry I don't have a guest room to offer you."

She lifted her head, and Chad caught his breath at the look in her eyes. They had darkened with an inner shadow that dimmed their brilliance. For a fanciful moment he imagined himself trapped within a murky forest glade untouched by sunlight, and suddenly he wanted to protect her from the darkness of her thoughts. No, he admitted wryly. It was his own selfishness she had to be protected from. As he had suspected from the beginning, Casey wasn't the type of woman to play games. When she had suggested that they come up here, she had been sincerely worried about him. She was not, as he had wanted to believe, willing to share her bed with him. The realization hit him with gut-wrenching intensity.

To his amazement, his physical reaction to her had been joined by a need to know this woman. Such a thing had never happened to him before. He felt light-headed as he looked at her, unfamiliar with the emotions rocketing through his body. There was almost a spiritual loveliness about her at this moment. She was reaching out to him in a way he didn't understand, but he knew he could never again ignore her needs or try to supplant them with his own.

"What are you thinking, Casey?" he whispered.

"I was wishing I'd been nicer to you when we first met."

His jaw tensed, and with an inner feeling of shame, he realized how jaded he had become in his relationships with women, jaded enough to view even Casey's gentle innocence with suspicion. "You have nothing to reproach yourself for." He walked past her to sit on the edge of the bed, bracing his elbows on his knees and staring down at his clasped hands. "But I do. Are you aware of what was on my mind when we walked up here?"

"I think so," she admitted gently. "But it wasn't your fault you thought I wanted you to make love to me. I . . . I shouldn't have grabbed at you like that."

He couldn't make himself look at her when he answered, even though she had moved to sit beside him. "I wanted to have sex with you. There is a difference, you know. In order to make love there has to be love. I've only had sex with women, Casey. From the moment we met I knew you were different," he muttered, the muscles in his arms contracting as he clenched his fists, "and yet I was afraid to admit it to myself, let alone to you."

He lifted his head, and his eyes met hers. "For the first time in my life I realize I don't know very much about loving, Casey."

"Then we're two of a kind," she remarked bitterly.

As he watched, her teeth savaged the inside of her mouth. She averted her eyes, as though unable to bear the sight of him. He was startled by the pain he felt at her evasion. "Look at me, Katherine!"

She obeyed his command, but her eyes were empty, her attention focused inward. Superimposed over Chad's features was another face, from another time. With the ear of memory she heard Hugh's voice again, harshly accusing as he condemned her lack of femininity.

"Holding you is like taking a mannequin in my arms," he accused, his glance derisive as he viewed her nakedness with disgusted thoroughness. "You have all the right equipment, but you haven't a clue how to use it."

Then teach me, her mind screamed. But she was incapable of uttering the silent cry. Instead she reached for the sheet with shaking hands, seeking only to hide herself from his eyes. "I can't force what I don't feel."

Hugh's laughter was bitter as he left her alone in the bed and moved toward his discarded clothing. Beginning to dress, he turned long enough to fix her with an unwavering stare. "I've heard that women suffering from frigidity can't fake it. Now I believe it!"

Casey, too, had believed. She had listened to the hollow echo of the front door slamming behind her husband, and she had believed. She learned of the mistress he made no effort to hide, and believed. She heard her husband demand a divorce, and believed. Until tonight, she had believed. But when Chad's mouth had brushed softly against her hair, a strange and wonderful metamorphosis had begun to take place in her unawakened body. Not since she was a child had she felt so right in a man's arms, and yet her emotions had hardly been child-like. She had wanted to press closer to him, to establish a more intimate contact.

"Poor Hugh," she sighed, regretting the fact that she had never felt such an awakening with her husband.

Chad turned and wrapped his fingers convulsively around the slender bones of her shoulders. The heated depth of his gaze drew her from the past with startling suddenness, and she flinched as she absorbed the warning in his eyes.

"Don't try to evade what's happening between

us, Katherine. There's no way you can run from either me or yourself, and using your ex-husband as a shield isn't the answer."

"It's what I'm used to."

"What in hell is that supposed to mean?"

She shrugged away his touch, and walked across the room. Her arms were wrapped across her chest as she stared out the window. Looking down, she saw curving, artfully lighted paths twisting among the postage-stamp lawns. The well-manicured trees and shrubs gave an illusion of openness to the grounds, while in reality they served to separate each condominium unit from the other as effectively as fences.

"I wanted freedom from the restrictions placed on me by my family," she whispered, "and I used Hugh to provide it. What does that make me, Chad?"

She braced herself inwardly when she heard his approach, but when he didn't try to touch her she sagged against the window frame. She waited for his condemnation the way she had so often waited for her husband's.

"Don't blame yourself, Casey. You thought you loved him at the time, didn't you?"

"Yes, but now I know I couldn't have," she said hollowly, aching with the pain of knowledge gained too late. "If I had, I would have felt something besides distaste when he touched me." She whirled around to face him, her features tortured. "Wouldn't I?"

"You really are innocent," he breathed, his

hands cupping her cheeks and holding her head still for his perusal. "What kind of a bumbling fool did you marry?"

"It wasn't his fault I was frigid!"

"If there's one thing I'm certain you're not, it's frigid."

Her mouth trembled, her eyes wide as she sought deliverance from a fear that had haunted her for years. "How can you possibly be sure of that?"

His smile didn't reach his eyes, but it nevertheless emphasized his sincerity. "I think you already know how, don't you, Katherine?"

She tensed, her gaze troubled, as her body once again began to respond to his closeness. She felt a liquid heat spread through her middle until it blazed a path through every inch of her body. Her nostrils inhaled his masculine scent with stunned pleasure, and the eyes that were trapped by his held bewilderment. "Hugh and I were married for nearly four years, and during all that time I couldn't lose myself in his arms. And yet with you I . . ." She closed her eyes, and bit down hard on her lower lip. "You're little more than a stranger, and yet I . . ."

"You want me?"

At the blunt certainty in his voice her eyes flew open, and she stared at him, shaking her head in denial. But she couldn't hold his gaze, and her head bowed in silent acknowledgment of the truth. She could protest from now until eternity, but she wouldn't be able to hide from the reality of what was happening between them. There were no words strong enough to deny their attraction to each other, and from the expression on his face she knew it would be useless to try.

"Don't be ashamed of the natural urgings of your body, Casey."

"I'm not ashamed," she whispered.

"Then why look as though you've been kicked in the stomach?"

"Because it's the way I feel," she cried, her features twisting. "One of the major problems in my marriage existed in the bedroom, and as long as I thought I couldn't help the way I felt, I didn't have to blame myself for the deterioration of our relationship."

"Don't you think it's time you stopped making yourself out the villain in your marriage?"

"I don't know what you mean," she replied mutinously.

He placed his finger beneath her chin and firmly tilted her head back until she was forced to meet his eyes. "How old was Hugh when you married?"

"What difference does that make?"

"How old, Casey?"

"He was twenty-eight, not that it's any of your business."

He ignored her sullenness. "Would you say he had some prior experience with women?"

She flushed, her lashes lowering as she tried to hide her embarrassment. "According to him he did," she remarked bitterly.

"Do you think it was simply empty boasting?"

She shook her head, fleeting pain darkening her

eyes. "His descriptions were too detailed to have been entirely false."

"Charming," Chad muttered in disgust, his features tightening with anger. "Yet you were a virgin when you married, weren't you?"

She jerked her head away from his cradling hand, and her eyes glittered with resentment as she glared at him. "Just what are you trying to prove?"

"Quite often certain types of men use ridicule to cover their own inadequacies, honey. I suspect your ex-husband was one of them. A man who's confident of his prowess in bed doesn't need to boast about former conquests to gain confidence in himself as a lover. If I'm right, then Hugh took advantage of your youth and inexperience. You didn't fail him as a woman, but he sure as hell failed you as a man!"

"But I didn't even try to make him happy," she moaned, tears beginning to shimmer in her eyes. "He was my husband. He had a right to be welcomed into his own bed."

With a low murmur of distress he drew her against him. "You speak of rights," he murmured, "as though sharing a man's bed was some kind of penance for being a woman. God, I could wring his bloody neck! Because you were never shown differently, to you making love is just a duty to be performed, isn't it, honey? If he'd loved you the way you deserve to be loved, you'd know the difference between lovemaking and empty sex."

"I thought you were the one who couldn't differentiate between the two, Chad."

He drew back to look at her. "I've always known there was a difference, but I've never experienced it. I've never found a woman who cared to be a friend as well as a lover. Will you be my friend, Katherine?"

Her eyes were solemn as she gazed at him. "I'll be your friend, but not your lover, Chad."

He closed his eyes briefly, and then nodded before walking with her to the door. "Good night, friend," he whispered, placing a gentle kiss on her forehead.

The flush of pleasure suffusing her face was reward enough for the man who watched her cross the hall. When she reached her bedroom door she turned, and he caught his breath at the sweetness of her smile.

"Good night," she responded shyly.

Casey was up early the next morning, happily humming an off-key tune while she moved around the kitchen. The thought of Chad's presence upstairs caused her to feel a lightness of spirit she hadn't experienced in too long a time to remember. It was nice to know there was another adult in the house, and even nicer knowing he was her friend. She prepared a pot of coffee, and opened the refrigerator door to inspect its contents. There was no bacon left, she remembered with a frown of annoyance. But she discovered onions and tomatoes in the vegetable bin. If she used her remaining cheese and eggs, she decided, she could cook up a mean omelet.

"What in the world are you doing, trying to climb inside that thing?" Chad spoke from the doorway, his voice husky with sleepiness.

Casey straightened, banging her head on the top rack of the refrigerator. She turned toward him with a grin and rubbed the injured spot. "Knowing you may prove injurious to my health. I thought *I* was the jinx."

He chuckled, and walked toward the coffeepot with a gleam of anticipation in his eyes. "Not any longer. I've decided you need a taste of your own medicine."

The words weren't even out of his mouth when the coffee he was pouring splattered, spraying his hand. By the time their laughter died, Casey was leaning weakly against the refrigerator, her hand braced on the door. "You were saying?"

"Don't get smart with me, woman, or I won't take you and Jon to breakfast."

"That's OK," she said, holding out a juicy red tomato for his inspection. "I'm going to fix you my specialty."

He eyed the round object in her hand. "Uhhh, Casey?"

"Hmmm?"

"I'm allergic to tomatoes."

She opened her mouth, then closed it again with a snap. "Why in heaven's name didn't you tell me? No wonder your stomach was bothering you last night."

"I didn't want to hurt your feelings."

"Chad, you're an idiot!"

He nodded, his lips pursing as he blew on his stinging hand. "That's why I'm so adorable."

"The word is stubborn," she laughed, replacing her rejected offering in the bin and closing the refrigerator door. "I'm starving! Let's go next door and pick up Jonathan."

He inspected the cup cradled between his palms, as though the design held a secret fascination for him. "I'll wait for you in my car."

"Don't be silly," she said, reaching the door and looking over her shoulder at him. "I'll probably be a while. Sally and I usually visit before I bring Jonathan home. She enjoys tempting me with gooey, homemade Danish."

Taking his assent for granted, she reached across the bar and unplugged the coffeepot. "Don't look so stricken," she giggled. "Sally will give you another cup."

Setting his cup in the sink, he joined her in front of the door. His impatience was plain as he looked down at her. "I'd still rather wait in the car."

She frowned. "I thought you liked Sally."

"Of course I do, it's just . . ." He inhaled, then harshly expelled the breath in his lungs. "I don't want her to know I spent the night here."

"Afraid for your reputation?" she teased.

"I'm afraid for yours," he admitted quietly.

Casey didn't hesitate. With a naturalness she didn't bother to question she moved into Chad's arms, and rested her cheek against his chest. The way she hugged his waist held no sexual implications; it was just an acknowledgment of gratitude.

Tightening his hold, Chad accepted the gift of her trust, and murmured, "I've never been protective of a woman before, little witch. I know the way I feel about you should scare the hell out of me, but do you know what?" He didn't wait for her answer. "It feels good, Katherine," he sighed, rubbing his chin against the top of her head. "It feels very, very good."

4

Are you going to eat that bacon, Casey?"

Casey finished wiping the last dribble of maple syrup from Jonathan's chin, and took amused note of the hungry expression on Chad's face as he eyed her plate. "Do you mean to tell me that after putting away three pancakes, toast, sausage, eggs, hashbrowns, and coffee, you're prepared to wage war over a piece of bacon?" She pushed her plate toward him, and shook her head in reproof. "You are a greedy man, Mr. Walker."

His eyes twinkled as he snatched up the bacon before she had a chance to change her mind. "I'm just being sensible, sweetheart. I'll need all my strength to deal with you."

He had taken a single bite when Jonathan said, "I like bacon, Chad."

With an exaggerated sigh of regret that made Jonathan giggle, Chad popped the remaining piece of bacon in the little boy's mouth, and rose to his feet. "The world's awaiting, sport. Come and help me pay the bill before your mother gets it in her head to suggest we go Dutch treat."

Casey looked suddenly guilty. "I don't see anything wrong with . . ."

"You see how it is, Jon?"

Chad placed his hand on Jonathan's head, and began to guide him in the right direction before Casey had a chance to finish her sentence. "Let that be a lesson to you. When you meet up with an independent woman, don't give her a chance to argue with you."

"What's Dutch treat, Chad?"

Casey grinned at the single-mindedness of Jonathan's questions. She knew her son, and when he started acquiring information his active brain could jump from one subject to the next with bewildering rapidity. By the end of the day, Chad was going to feel as mentally limp as a wet dishrag, she thought, feeling not a bit guilty for finding pleasure in the prospect. It would serve him right for daring to enlist Jonathan's support. Independent woman, indeed!

But by the end of the day, it wasn't Chad who was teetering on the edge of exhaustion. Nor was he limp from answering Jonathan's questions. Casey's head ached, her feet ached, and her body felt as though she'd been trampled by a herd of rhinoceroses. They had certainly stared at the ugly horned beasts long enough, she thought. After making a brief stop at his motel so Chad could shower and change, they had headed for the Knowland Zoo.

Chad and Jonathan had proceeded to circle the park three times, while she hobbled along behind on burning feet, before they ensconced themselves in the baby petting zoo, much to Jonathan's delight. To give Chad his due, he had been solicitous of her comfort throughout the day. But the deviltry in his eyes every time he asked her if she'd had enough only increased her determination not to give in. She wasn't about to accept his ribbing if she proved unequal to the challenge. She'd show him she was no delicate bit of fluff!

The fourth time Chad caught her looking enviously at Jonathan as he sat perched on his broad shoulders, he began to head for the exit. She groaned with relief as she spotted his car. "You're a plucky little chicken, aren't you?" he asked, handing her the keys to unlock the passenger door.

"My mommy's not a chicken," Jonathan protested, giggling when he was flipped forward and deposited in the backseat.

"No, that's certainly not what I feel like at the moment," Casey admitted, returning Chad's keys and easing herself into the car without further discussion. She was certain both Chad and Jonathan could hear her bones creak as she leaned back against the sun-warmed bucket seat. She slipped out of her dusty sandals and wriggled her toes.

After joining them in the car, Chad glanced back

at Jonathan. His chest rumbled with laughter when he asked, "Why don't we ask Mommy what kind of an animal she feels like, Jon?"

The small boy began bouncing on his knees, his hands clutching the headrest as he eagerly threw himself into the fray. "A puppy . . . a puppy," he squealed eagerly. "I like puppies!"

"Well, Mommy," Chad drawled, leaning across the console divider to brush back a strand of Casey's hair. "What's it to be?"

"A jackass wouldn't be far off the mark."

Jonathan's voice held reproach. "That's a bad word, Mommy!"

Chad decided to protect her image in her son's eyes, and as they drove over the hills toward home Casey learned more about jackasses than she'd ever expected to know. She closed her eyes and relaxed in the late afternoon heat that filtered into the car. Her voice was drowsy as she broke into the discussion long enough to compliment Chad on the car he was driving.

"It's just a rental, but if you like the make, I'll buy one like it. What's your favorite color?"

Her smile widened as she lied with relish. "Pink."

It was hard to be certain with closed eyes, but from the choking sounds Chad was making she could almost bet his color was high. Men with hair as fair as his usually reddened easily when enraged. Unable to resist temptation, she wriggled herself into position and carefully lifted one lid. She was immediately intrigued by a tiny dimple that was visible in his cheek.

When she realized his silence hadn't been caused by shock, she was momentarily disgruntled. If first impressions were anything to go by, Chad was having great difficulty controlling his amusement. She scowled and opened her eyes. "What's so funny?"

"I was just trying to picture your face when I show up at your place driving a pink Mercedes."

"You wouldn't dare!"

His eyes met hers briefly. "To please you I'd do damned near anything," he murmured.

She caught her breath as she stared at the tender expression on his face. Her heartbeat thundered in her ears when she realized how badly she wanted to trace his mouth with her fingers. But when she lifted her gaze, there was nothing boyish about the expression in his eyes. She quickly turned her head and pretended an interest in the passing scenery. They might be friends, she thought nervously, but he wasn't about to let her forget he was also a man.

Realizing Casey was disturbed by the unexpected intimacy between them, he asked, "How about stopping for dinner in Dublin?"

"Need I remind you that the three of us smell like the baby goats you insisted we carry around most of the day?"

He looked inordinately pleased at the reminder. "I've always loved small animals. Anyway, it's as good a way as any to ensure privacy."

"It's also a good way to make certain the waitress doesn't show up with the food."

Casey needn't have worried. Chad bypassed

Dublin and pulled into a chain restaurant where anyone wearing shoes and a shirt would be given a table. For the most part, she noted with relief, their fellow diners weren't in much better shape than they were. When one young mother slipped her wailing toddler's shoe off and shook sand onto the carpet, Casey grinned in sympathy and slid into a corner booth.

She soon discovered that a trip to the baby zoo hadn't diminished Chad's ability to charm. He couldn't have kept their waitress away if he'd tried. On the contrary, she hovered throughout their meal. Casey was enjoying herself too much to count the times Chad glanced warily in her direction. Clearly, he was embarrassed by the attention he was being paid.

She took a large bite of her hamburger, chewing and swallowing automatically while she absorbed his embarrassment. "You're a very persuasive, charming man, aren't you, blue eyes?"

His color rose, but he responded to her teasing calmly. "I don't know," he remarked, surveying her features with interest. "Am I?"

She nodded, her eyes sparkling. "But don't let it go to your head. Pride goeth before a fall."

He leaned forward and rested his arms beside his plate. He was wearing a gold knit sport shirt with short sleeves, and she was distracted by the contrast between his softly glinting blond hair and his bronzed flesh. "Since I've already fallen, sweetness, your warning's a little late," he drawled.

Darting a quick look at his face, she blushed.

Such gorgeous, mesmerizing blue eyes, she mused, hurriedly reaching for her water glass. When it toppled over, leaving a puddle on their table, she stared at her hand with exasperation while Chad chuckled and wiped up the spill. "How does it feel to be on the receiving end, little witch?"

"If I'm a witch, you show every indication of being a warlock."

He nodded confidently. "Now you know we were meant for each other."

"What's a warlock, Mommy?" Jonathan mumbled, his question nearly indecipherable due to the mouthful of french fries he was trying to chew.

She found the distraction too welcome to bother scolding him for talking with his mouth full, and instead satisfied her motherly urges by wiping a smear of catsup from his cheek. Jonathan was waiting for an answer, and since she never purposely evaded the truth when dealing with his myriad questions, she gave him a rather abbreviated and vague definition. She didn't want to come right out and say a warlock was a male witch. It was bad enough that she wove fantasies around Chad without having her son starting to visualize him as some kind of a superman. "A warlock is the counterpart of a witch."

She should have known better than to hope it would end there. Jonathan swallowed, looked from her to Chad, and frowned suspiciously. "What's counterpart mean?"

Casey looked helplessly in Chad's direction, and with a smile he responded to her unspoken plea for assistance. "One of the dictionary definitions is, 'two parts that fit.'"

Jonathan cocked his head as he assimilated the information. "Do you and Mommy fit together, Chad?"

Casey choked on a sip of Coke, and glared at Chad. Before she could say a word, he had covered his face with his hands. She was becoming quite irritated by his suppressed hilarity, and if Jonathan asked one more question, she was going to smack him. With an exasperated cry she slid out of her seat and practically dragged the bewildered little boy after her.

Guiding her son toward the ladies' room, she hesitated long enough to sneak a quick glance over her shoulder before rounding the corner of their booth. Chad's shoulders were still shaking, and the sounds emerging from his mouth made her long to gag him.

Casey pulled open the heavy door of the rear entrance of "A Touch of Italy," and winced at the pain that pierced her spine. It was her own fault her back was out of joint, she thought in disgust. Hard work was one way of killing time, as she had learned during the past few days. She hadn't seen Chad since he had taken Jonathan and herself to the zoo, and she had never dreamed a week could pass so slowly. The day after their outing, he had been unexpectedly summoned to his Los Angeles office, and as one day followed another with monotonous regularity, she found herself missing him

unbearably. No matter how many times she be-
rated herself for letting his absence figure so largely
in her mind, she couldn't seem to stop thinking
about him.

Not that he returned the favor, she thought
angrily. Other than one phone call at the beginning
of the week, she hadn't heard from him. At first she
had imagined all sorts of dire calamities. She was
relieved when no plane crashes were reported on
the news, but that didn't rule out a car accident, a
virus, appendicitis . . . the possibilities were endless. But before long she began to view her exces-
sive concern with irony. The one possibility she
hadn't wanted to consider was that Chad was using
this method to distance himself from her. Well, he
needn't be afraid of her becoming possessive, she
thought indignantly. The last person she wanted or
needed in her life was Mr. Chad Walker!

Casey mumbled an indistinct imprecation under
her breath as she stepped into the kitchen, her
mind preoccupied with trying to remember her
chiropractor's phone number. She had a better
than average memory and ordinarily would have
had no difficulty bringing the required numerals
quickly to mind. She'd dialed it often enough to
have it down pat, she thought, scowling blackly as
she hurried around the stainless-steel counter. But
it wasn't until she heard Marilyn's voice wishing her
a good evening that she realized the significance of
the numbers crowding her mind. Two-four-two-
three . . . C-H-A-D!

Her voice was indignant when she snapped, "What's good about it?"

"Uh, is something bothering you, Casey?"

"Weren't you the one who played matchmaker and introduced me to that damn man, you . . . you Judas?"

"It's a little late to be telling me I put my foot in it, isn't it?"

"Both feet," Casey hissed, with saccharine sweetness, "as well as your mouth!"

"But Casey, I thought you and Chad were getting along fine together."

"We are not . . . getting along . . . fine," Casey emphasized carefully.

"You've had a little misunderstanding?"

"If he were here, I'd wring his neck," she announced with relish, the light of battle in her eyes.

"'Atta girl," Marilyn crowed, clapping her hands together. "You go ahead and give as good as you get. It'll serve him right to be strung out and hung up to dry, the beast!"

Marilyn hesitated, a frown creasing her brow. "Casey?"

"What?"

Marilyn's frown deepened into a worried furrow. "What did he do?"

Sharon bustled into the kitchen, taking in Casey's tight-lipped expression at a glance. "If Marilyn's done anything to upset you, Casey, I'll brain her with that bucket in the corner."

Casey's smile was strained. "I'm not really mad at Marilyn, just the world in general."

"And one person in particular," Marilyn muttered, clamping her mouth shut as she received a warning glance from Casey.

But Sharon was nobody's fool, and she glanced from her sister to Casey with speculation darkening her eyes. "I take it this Chad you've told me about is the culprit?" she asked Marilyn.

Marilyn nodded, and pushed herself onto the top of a convenient counter. "He's in trouble with Casey at the moment, and I'm getting the brunt of it."

"What do you have to do with anything?" Sharon asked, suspicion in her eyes as she studied her sister. "Have you been sticking your nose in where it doesn't belong again?"

"All I did was introduce them," Marilyn protested, stiffening with indignation. "It's not my fault if that wonderfully wicked male broke through Casey's defenses." She sent Sharon a look that spoke volumes. "She was just about to tell me what was wrong when you butted in."

Ignoring the jibe, Sharon turned her attention to Casey. "Marilyn described Chad to me. He must be quite a man."

Marilyn sighed expressively, and rolled her eyes. "He's a hunk!"

Casey fixed Marilyn with a reproving stare. "Are men the only thing you think about?"

The other woman managed to achieve an innocent smile. "Unlike certain people I could mention," she said, her glance encompassing both Casey and Sharon, "I do much more than think about the gorgeous creatures."

Casey sniffed and shook her head in reproof. "That's the reason you associate them with trouble, you idiot. If you'd learn the benefits of abstinence, you wouldn't end up hurting so often."

Marilyn waved a negligent hand, the scarlet tips of her fingernails slicing the air for emphasis as she declared dramatically, "I would think myself dead, *cara*."

A flicker of distress showed in Casey's eyes, and Marilyn pursed her lips in determination as she viewed her friend's troubled expression. "Our Mr. Walker has managed to crack the great wall, hasn't he, Casey?"

Casey nodded her head mutely, her expression so woebegone that Marilyn burst into laughter. "Then why the sad look?" she demanded. "There's nothing wrong with our little Jonathan, is there?"

"No, he's fine, but . . ."

". . . and you haven't found cockroaches in your cupboards?"

Casey bit her lip to stop herself from smiling, and shook her head in exasperation. "No, it's nothing like that, but . . ."

"Will you two please let me in on this one-sided conversation?" Sharon demanded.

With a wry twist to her lips Casey joined Marilyn on top of the butcher-block cutting table occupying the center of the cavernous kitchen. She nearly groaned at the hurt look in Sharon's eyes. The sisters resembled each other strongly, and yet they were as different as chalk and cheese, she thought. Sharon's slightly plumper frame and booming voice, a carry-over from a ten-year stint in the army, often led strangers to view her as the more sensible of the two. Yet Casey knew it was Sharon who had the more vulnerable personality. Marilyn hid a practical streak a mile wide beneath her devil-may-care facade, while Sharon's no-nonsense manner disguised the heart of a true romantic.

"Casey, are you being deliberately irritating?" Marilyn asked.

Marilyn's eyes flashed with impatience, but Sharon placed a restraining hand on her sister's arm. "Casey has a right to her privacy," she said. "If she wants us to know anything, she'll tell us."

"You know I'd never keep anything from either of you," Casey said, her reserve finally breaking down. "Just don't make a big deal out of this, all right?"

Two heads bobbed in unison, and, with an inward sigh at their hopeful expressions, Casey began to explain the reason for her anger. "If he's thought twice about our friendship," she concluded, "then he should have had the decency to tell me so to my face!"

Marilyn pursed her lips in a low whistle. "You've really been jumping to conclusions."

"I'm simply being a realist," Casey retorted stiffly. "I have no intention of going to bed with the man, and he knows it. He probably decided I wasn't worth his time, and went on to an easier conquest."

Sharon cleared her throat. "If Chad is important to you, shouldn't you give him a chance to explain, Casey?"

"I couldn't care less if I never saw him again!"

Casey carefully masked a twinge of pain at the thought. Before either of the other women could remark on the desolate tone of her voice, she jumped down from the wooden counter. "Isn't it time to feed the starving masses?"

Marilyn reacted to the deliberate change of topic with a grin. "Don't we wish."

Sharon stretched, and headed for the swinging doors that divided the kitchen from the restaurant. "Would you finish setting up the bar for me while I unlock the front doors, Casey?"

Worrisome thoughts followed Casey into the washroom, where she listlessly exchanged her jeans and tank top for the white, off-the-shoulder ruffled blouse and full, brightly colored knee-length skirt that served as the standard uniform for the waitresses at A Touch of Italy.

She was depressed by the lack of logic in her behavior. She didn't want her life to be complicated by a relationship with Chad, and yet she couldn't help feeling hurt by his defection.

She tightened the belt at her waist with a vicious tug. Stepping into her low-heeled sandals, she grimaced into the mirror hanging haphazardly against the wall. The slightly tilted glass reflected her flushed features with unerring accuracy, while the glaring overhead light bulb revealed the feverish glitter in her eyes. She wanted to wipe Chad's memory from her mind, and yet she found she couldn't block out even one detail of their time together. She remembered the way those blue eyes of his had effortlessly reduced her to a creature of uninhibited sensuality. She remembered the texture of his hair beneath her hands and the vibrant timbre of his voice when he spoke to her.

On the whole, she remembered too damn much, she decided. Making up her mind to banish Chad Walker from her thoughts, at least for one evening, she threw open the washroom door and headed for the central area of the restaurant. Her pulse thundered in her head, one of the symptoms of the migraine headaches she'd suffered in the months following her divorce. She had thought the headaches to be a thing of the past, brought on by tension and uncertainty, but the pain she was now experiencing proved her wrong.

Suppressing a groan, she walked through the dining room and into the bar. She was imagining things, she told herself staunchly. Her aching head had nothing to do with that irritating man. Her back was out of place; that was the only reason for her headache. It wasn't uncertainty about Chad that made her tense. She knew right where he belonged in her life . . . and that was out of it.

It was a shame she couldn't make herself believe what she was thinking.

Her hands were trembling as she wiped down

the bar. A satisfying influx of customers began to fill the restaurant, and several gravitated in her direction to wait until they could be seated at a table. Keeping busy had tremendous therapeutic value, and she smiled as she took their orders. The smile remained glued to her face even when a florid-faced gentleman on her left attempted to flirt with her.

"You don't look old enough to be working behind a bar," he said, but his jocularity faltered when Casey glanced impersonally in his direction.

She caught a blur of movement out of the corner of her eye. Before she could focus on the new arrival, the drink she'd just given her annoying customer slipped from his hand. The pungent odor of whiskey permeated both the air and her admirer. But at least the man was no longer leering at her. He was too busy wiping his pants.

She mopped up the spill with stoic resignation, then bent to drop the soiled rag into the basin under the bar. She was just starting to rise when a laughing voice offered a greeting.

"I've missed you, little witch."

5

Chad's eyes followed Casey while she straightened. Her features had a pinched look as she stared back at him, and he noticed how tightly her hands were wrapped around the edge of the bar. His brow creased in concern as she lifted trembling fingers to her temples. "Casey, are you all right?"

Her lashes fluttered in a brief moment of indecision before she gave full reign to her indignation. "It's just a headache. I've been under something of a strain the last few days, wondering about the well-being of a friend of mine." She sniffed disdainfully, and stared at him accusingly. "Some friend!"

He winced, his eyes rueful as he noted her anger. "I'm sorry you were worried."

"Why should I worry about you, Chad Walker? You're old enough to take care of yourself."

"All right, maybe my choice of an adjective wasn't quite accurate. I ran into Sally before coming here. According to her you were frantic when you didn't hear from me, and for that I apologize. My only defense was my eagerness to be with you again. I crammed a week's worth of meetings into the last few days so I could get back to you."

There was a comically penitent expression on his face. "Are you going to stay mad at me for long? I hope not, because I'm aching for a kiss hello. If the frown on that little mouth of yours is anything to go by, though, it looks like I've got my work cut out for me. But my mother always told me 'Where there's a will, there's a way,' Casey. I have a very strong will, so be warned. Finding a way has never been much of a problem for me, either."

"You can just forget any welcome back kisses," she said, deliberately tightening her lips. She was angry with herself for allowing his explanation to allay her original feeling of grievance. "I'm amazed I'm even speaking to you!"

"I thought we were friends."

"In my opinion you're taking friendship a little too far."

At the coolness in her voice he shrugged. "What are you going to do when I decide to add a little more warmth to our relationship, Casey? Run for the hills?"

Irritation strengthened her voice as she fixed him with a mutinous glance. "That decision isn't entirely yours to make. I've made my wishes on that score plain, Chad. Just what do you hope to achieve by pursuing me this way?"

He reacted to her question with assumed indifference, only the merest flicker of emotion showing in his gaze as he slowly ran his eyes over her slight figure. But by the time his wandering glance returned to her face, there was a fire in his eyes that left Casey in no doubt as to what he eventually wanted from her.

"You know the answer to that as well as I do, Katherine."

How could she not know, when he'd just been reinforcing his claim on her? She had never had much of a problem dissuading other men from having more than a fleeting interest in pursuing a relationship with her, she thought in frustration. Why was she having so much trouble discouraging this obstinate male? Because this is the first time you've had to fight your own desires, too, Casey, her conscience whispered. His certainty that they would become lovers left her shaken. When he looked at her he didn't fantasize about lovemaking —he made it!

Despite herself she responded to the almost palpable touch of his eyes—and he knew it. Tonight a new element was being added to their relationship, a tentative but mutual admission of the sensual tension between them. There was no longer any point in cloaking their attraction to each other beneath the guise of friendship. With totally masculine confidence in his persuasive abilities Chad was determined to forge a place for himself in her life. It was as though having gotten under her skin, he was now going in search of her soul. He saw too much that she wanted to keep hidden, and, like a helpless animal captured by a tiger, she felt a primitive need to survive.

When Marilyn turned from seating a party of four and sauntered over to stand beside Chad, Casey was glad for the interruption at first. But after several minutes, she felt oddly at a loss as to how to cope with the easy camaraderie between Marilyn and Chad. A part of her wanted him to walk away and never come back; the desire was so strong it was like an acrid taste on her tongue. She didn't want to share her friends or any other aspect of her life with him. But there was another voice inside of her, one she didn't want to acknowledge. It was this taunting part of her psyche that made her realize that when Chad eventually left her, he would be leaving her lonelier than she'd ever been before.

As she moved down the bar to attend to her customers she looked back at Chad, who was listening to Marilyn with an intent expression on his face. He exuded self-confidence and a devastating masculine charm that made Casey uneasy. His attractiveness was a very definite threat to her peace of mind, and she resented him for making her feel drawn to him. He was dangerous, she thought, as she admitted to herself how easily he had broken through her protective shell.

Just watching him talking to Marilyn created an appalling feeling of insecurity inside her. Marilyn was her friend, and she didn't want Chad's presence intruding on that friendship. She busied herself at the bar with shaking hands, automatically replacing drinks and making change without the least idea of what she was doing. To her disgust, her attention never wavered from Chad.

She wondered what Chad and Marilyn were discussing with such pleasure, and suddenly was envious of the easy rapport between them. A twisting sensation in her chest made her cover the furiously pounding pulse in her throat with her hand. She hadn't thought herself capable of such intense emotion. She was jealous, and it was all she could do not to make a fool of herself. She wanted to insert herself between them, demanding their attention. Oh, Lord, she thought wearily, to think that she would come to this!

When she had calmed herself sufficiently to rejoin them, she heard Marilyn remark, "I never thought I'd see the day when Casey lost sleep over any man."

"Marilyn, shouldn't you be getting back to work?" Casey hissed, resisting the urge to cover her friend's mouth with her hand.

With airy unconcern Marilyn glanced toward the buildup of clientele spilling over from the hallway into the lounge. "You're right, Casey. I should return to my duties as hostess before Sharon comes at me with a meat cleaver." Turning to Chad, she smiled disarmingly. "I've enjoyed our little chat enormously. I'm sure we'll be seeing a lot more of you from now on."

"You can bet on it, Marilyn."

In Casey's opinion his assertion was made with more emphasis than the situation warranted. A grin practically split his face as he watched the other woman's hips sway seductively in the direction of her waiting customers. "She's quite a gal, your friend. She cares for you and Jonathan a great deal."

Casey sniffed, her eyes shooting daggers at Marilyn's retreating back. "Too much at times!"

Casey discovered the true meaning of endurance as she struggled through the next few hours. No matter how busy she kept herself, she never lost her awareness of Chad's presence. Some of her tension subsided when Irene, their most experienced waitress, arrived to take over as bartender. As usual, Irene's mouth began working as swiftly as her hands, and Casey used the distraction the waitress provided to move from behind the bar.

When Chad swiveled around on his stool to study her departure with amused eyes, her hope of disappearing into the kitchen unnoticed died. Of necessity she had to navigate around his lounging figure, and although she used extraordinary care not to brush up against him, disaster struck when he shifted to stretch his legs. His heavy leather boot connected with the toe of her sandal and she pitched forward into his waiting arms.

"Does this mean I've been forgiven?"

The sensual rasp in her ear brought her survival instincts to the fore, but being cradled between Chad's muscular thighs somewhat diminished her fighting spirit. When those hard thighs contracted to restricting bands against her legs, she lost track of everything but the warm body that seemed to envelope her. Their glances locked in awareness, she was powerless to break away from the possessive gleam in his eyes.

Those eyes were now zeroing in on her mouth with the precision of a laser. When his head began to descend, she froze. Her hands formed fists against his chest, and yet she couldn't seem to find the willpower to stave off the inevitable. Slowly her fingers opened and began to move in a tentative search across his shirt. Her awareness of the people around them began to recede, until their voices held no more ability to intrude on her preoccupation with Chad than the buzzing of flies.

A titter of laughter sounded from over Chad's shoulder, and Casey's eyes flew open in horrified realization. Dazedly, she became aware of Irene's curious gaze, and it proved the impetus Casey needed to break free of Chad's arms.

"For heaven's sake, Chad!"

He groaned and released her with reluctance. "For my sake, Casey?"

She stepped back and nervously began to smooth out the wrinkles in her skirt. "This is hardly the time or the place."

"Then I'll have to be patient until later if I expect to collect that kiss you owe me, won't I?"

She didn't respond . . . she couldn't. She stumbled across the foyer with a lurching gait. Apparently he intended to wait for her whether she wanted him to or not. When Chad made up his mind about something, she thought groggily, he went after what he wanted with deadly efficiency. As she began to feverishly take orders for meals, refill coffee cups, and generally see to the comfort of their dinner clientele, she could feel his eyes following her around the room.

Although busy taking yet another order through to the kitchen, Casey was aware of the exact moment Chad dropped a tip on the bar and rose to his feet. Her heart pounded sickeningly as he stretched his long body with easy grace. She couldn't seem to tear her eyes away and she felt her knees weaken just looking at him. The fabric of his shirt tightened over the bulging muscles of his chest, and as the stretch arched his back, his firm hips jutted forward slightly. The movement was so unconsciously sensual, she forgot to breathe.

"Hey, are you okay?"

The busboy's voice reverberated in her eardrum, increasing the throb of her migraine. She felt his steadying hand on her arm through a blur of pain and found it impossible to answer. He led her out of the dining room to one of the cushioned settees in the empty lounge area. Leaning her head back, she tried to smile at the worried youngster with reassurance. But Johnny's freckled face was minus its usual animation as he took in the paleness of Casey's cheeks.

She had been responsible for hiring Johnny in a part-time capacity, and he remained endearingly loyal. Although Marilyn had been dubious about the staying power of a sixteen-year-old junior in high school, Johnny had never once abused Casey's trust in him. He was unfailingly punctual, conscientious, and quite adult in his ambition to help his parents with his upcoming college tuition. Much to Casey's usual amusement and current irritation, he also tended to be overprotective. Right now, as the ache in her back merged with the knife thrusts of pain in her head, she was beyond humor.

"Is your back out again, Casey?"

The words were no sooner out of Johnny's mouth than she sensed another presence. With more effort than the action warranted she squinted up to see who it was. Her vision was blurred, and she groaned when one austerely scowling face divided itself into two. One Chad was bad enough, she thought. All she needed now was to be confronted by his twin!

"Come on, Casey. I'm taking you home."

Another set of footsteps tapped out a hurried rhythm against the tile floor, and Marilyn's voice joined that of Johnny as she questioned Chad. Casey tried to tell Marilyn that she was fine, but couldn't call forth the effort it took to speak. Even when Chad lifted her to her feet, she found herself without the strength to do more than mumble a disgustingly weak protest.

"Shut up," Chad responded, his well-modulated voice pleasant.

"You are not a nice man," she complained, sighing with relief when his long strides hurried them through the door Johnny held open and into the cool air of late evening. Marilyn trailed along behind them into the parking lot.

"Such a clever woman you are," he said, his eyes glittering in the light from the dashboard as he deposited her in his car. "What are you trying to prove by pushing yourself so hard?"

"It's called working to pay the bills."

She winced as she tried to relax her back against the supple upholstery of the bucket seat. The movement caused excruciating pain to shoot up from between her shoulder blades, and moisture beaded her upper lip as she fought back a wave of nausea.

"Casey, what is it?" Marilyn cried, stretching to see over Chad's shoulder. "Is it your back?"

"I heard the busboy ask her the same question," Chad said, fastening the seat belt around Casey's waist and straightening to face Marilyn. "Does this happen often?"

"She throws it out occasionally, and then there's hell to pay," Marilyn explained, reaching over to smooth Casey's hair in sympathy. "Why didn't you tell us? There was no need to suffer in silence like this."

Casey managed to reply with a little coherency despite the jumble of her thoughts. "We had a full house in there tonight, and I knew you needed me to help."

"Oh, Casey," Marilyn wailed. "When are you going to stop putting everyone else first?"

Chad spoke quietly as he walked around to the driver's side, but there was a grim inflection in his voice. "As of right now, Marilyn. I'll call and let you know how she is later. First I'm taking her to see a doctor."

As the car pulled out of the parking area, Casey inwardly cursed her helplessness. Nine o'clock at night was definitely not within normal clinic visiting hours, and Chad was sensibly heading in the direction of the hospital. All she needed to end this disastrous day was another visit to the emergency room, she thought glumly. Summoning the last of her flagging strength, she tried to reason with the stubborn man at her side. "I don't need a doctor, Chad."

"Don't argue," he growled, giving her a disgusted look. His impatience changed to nervousness as he noted the moisture on her skin. "Give me a little warning if you think you're going to be sick, and I'll pull over."

"Now who's preoccupied with throwing up?"

"Don't be cute, Katherine. I'm not in the mood."

Casey carefully turned her head and lifted her lashes far enough to observe his worried features. His mouth was tightly compressed, and she felt a strong urge to smooth away the tension in his jaw with her fingers. Instead she gripped her hands together in her lap and sought to ease the strained silence growing between them with an apology.

"I'm sorry, Chad. I've got one terrific headache, but I've had them before."

"More reason to see a doctor."

The contrition she felt at causing him worry immediately evaporated at his high-handedness.

"Backache often causes headaches from compressed nerves. I'm not going to swallow painkillers when my chiropractor can probably solve the problem instantly. He works out of his home and often takes emergency calls."

Chad's sigh, expressing an equal degree of resignation and exasperation, made her smile. "How do I get there?"

"Is your headache any better, honey?"

Casey stepped through the door Chad held open for her and entered the comforting familiarity of her living room. Dropping her purse onto the coffee table, she stifled a yawn with the back of her hand. "Mmmm, it's much better," she admitted, slipping out of her sweater and depositing it next to her purse. "Those muscle relaxants Charlie made me take did the trick."

"Made you is right!" Chad shook his head ruefully. "I could hear you arguing with him while I paced the waiting room."

"Why in the world were you pacing? Charlie was just adjusting my bones, not cutting into my innards."

"I didn't like the idea of some strange man fooling around with your bones."

Her laughter rippled out. "Charlie's not strange."

"Is that why you looked so revitalized when you came out, because you enjoyed deafening the poor guy?"

Casey grinned. "Charlie would be very disappointed in me if I started acting like a meek little woman. Anyway, that was only a loud discussion you heard. I never argue."

"Then come here," he whispered.

Her eyes widened warily. "Why?"

She knew why very well. The sensual slant of his mouth ridiculed her resistance, and she tilted her chin defiantly. "You stay right where you are, Chad Walker!"

His laughter followed her as she darted across the room and entered the kitchen. "I thought you said you never argue, Katherine?"

Wanting to kick herself for inadvertently allowing their conversation to develop into intimacy, Casey avoided a reply. Instead she reached into the cupboard for a glass and tried to regain a little control while she listened to Chad rummaging around in the bathroom medicine cabinet. Whatever it is he's looking for, she thought nervously, I hope it takes him a long time to find it. Her prayer went unanswered; Chad entered the kitchen from the doorway nearest the bathroom with a smile curving his mouth. Casey immediately turned to fill the glass she held with water, all the while watching him warily from out of the corner of her eye. The clear, cool liquid eased the dryness in her throat, but couldn't do a thing to prevent her feeling irritated by his relaxed attitude.

He moved to lean against the counter, his arm resting on the pale green Formica-topped surface. He had unbuttoned the cuffs of his shirt and rolled the material as far as his elbows, and she was disturbed by the sight of his hard, sinewy flesh. His eyes followed her movements with exaggerated interest, and when he straightened and began to shift in her direction she could feel her body tense in readiness.

"Take two of these while you're at it."

She stared down at the small white pills resting in his palm in chagrined surprise. She felt like a fool for mentally preparing herself to resist his sensual appeal when all he'd had in mind was having her take the aspirin Charlie had prescribed.

"I don't need them, Chad."

Casey winced at the petulance in her voice. Her embarrassment caused a hot flush to suffuse her skin as she stared at his chest. For the first time she noticed he had removed his tie and loosened the top three buttons of his shirt. His muscular chest was visible in the opening, and her attention fixed on the curling tufts of blond hair in the vee. Hurriedly she lifted the nearly forgotten glass to her mouth. She should have known better than to trust her body to cooperate. The water caught somewhere between the back of her tongue and her Adam's apple, and the coughing that ensued did nothing to aid her composure. It didn't help when Chad, conscious of her sore muscles, began to run his hand in a circular motion between her shoulder blades.

Even through the protective covering of her blouse she felt a tingling sensation from his touch, and as her coughing subsided she wondered how his naked hand would feel against her flesh.

Shocked by the ache of longing that leaped like fire through her veins, she twisted to escape his ministrations. She was immediately aware of the rashness of her action and gasped in pain as her back protested the sudden movement.

"That tears it," Chad muttered, taking the glass from her hand before she had a chance to spill the liquid down the front of his slacks.

Her laughter sounded pathetic to her own ears as she braced her palms against the edge of the sink. "That's about what it feels like."

The shrill peal of the telephone interrupted them, but before Casey had a chance to straighten, Chad had already lifted the receiver and uttered a distracted greeting. When his expression of bland politeness changed to one of brooding impatience, she was filled with a presentiment of disaster. Slowly she moved to stand beside him, and his eyes held subdued rage as he offered her the phone. "Your ex-husband doesn't bother with the niceties, does he? As soon as I opened my mouth he demanded to speak to you. Shall I hang up?"

She brushed a nervous hand over her hair and shook her head. Of all the times for Hugh to call, she thought, he would pick tonight! But Hugh's rudeness to a guest wasn't the only thing she was finding irritating at the moment. Chad's aggressive stance at her side didn't bear close inspection, either. He was acting as if she was the one responsible for the call, when in reality the last thing she wanted to do was chat with her former spouse. If

Chad's opinion was anything to judge by, Hugh probably wasn't in a very sociable mood.

Well, she wasn't in the best frame of mind herself. With an exasperated exclamation she turned and lifted the receiver to her mouth. Although she stared over her shoulder at Chad, he refused to withdraw and give her any privacy. His good humor seemingly restored by her reluctance to speak to the man waiting on the other end of the line, he bent down and began to nuzzle the top of her head. She suspected Chad's muffled laughter was meant as a deliberate affront to Hugh, and she shoved her elbow into his side after belatedly covering the receiver with her hand. Her voice was far from cordial when she greeted Hugh.

"Casey, who the hell was that on the phone?"

"A friend," she remarked defensively. "Isn't it rather late for you to be calling me?"

"Isn't it rather late to be entertaining friends?" he rejoined sarcastically.

"My life is my own, Hugh," she began belligerently, then suddenly drew in her breath with a dismayed gasp. She hadn't heard from him in months, but in less than two minutes she was allowing him to pressure her into justifying her behavior. Where was the veneer of confidence she'd learned to arm herself with in the months since their divorce? She felt panic steal over her as she remembered the full extent of her ex-husband's dominance in the past.

She was aware that Chad's body had tensed at

the ill-disguised panic in her tone, and she struggled to compose herself. When his bold mouth wandered to her temple, she found it almost impossible to formulate any coherent thoughts. Lowering her head to evade his lips, she tried again to discover Hugh's reason for calling.

The laughter that resulted from her question held more insinuation than amusement. "Why don't I save my explanations for when we're together again, hmmm?"

"What do you mean?"

Casey didn't need Chad's abrupt scowl to tell her she was losing her cool. She was shocked by the shrillness of her own voice and quickly tried to control the dread she felt at Hugh's words. Hugh was annoyed by her bluntness and, as usual in his dealings with Casey, he didn't try to hide his petulance.

"I mean I'm coming home to you and Jonathan."

Casey's breath rushed into her lungs. "You might be returning to California, but you are not returning to us, Hugh."

"You sound very sure of yourself, but I know better, Casey. Just because you've found yourself a little playmate, please don't imagine I'll lie down and let you walk all over me. I will be returning to California soon, and we'll discuss our future when I get there."

"We have no future," she hissed.

He wasn't listening to a word she said, and she was damned if she was going to let him get away with his bullying tactics. She'd had enough of that during their marriage, she thought, her hand tightening around the receiver until her knuckles blanched. "Did you hear me, Hugh?"

She was answered by a dial tone. "Damn," she muttered.

She slammed the phone in its cradle violently. She had completely forgotten Chad's interest in the conversation until she heard him utter an imprecation beneath his breath. She looked up, and the sympathy in his expression was nearly her undoing.

"Can I help, Casey?"

Fighting angry tears, she shook her head and tried to smile for his benefit. "I can handle him on my own, but thanks for the offer."

"Are you sure you're not going to need me to run interference?"

This time her smile held real amusement. "Is that how you broke your nose?"

At the abrupt change of subject he grinned and fingered the bump on his nose. "I wasn't up to my usual weight." He paused, his eyes narrowing. "I only hope you are, honey."

This time her eyes were infused with the strength of inner certainty. "I'll go down fighting before I'll let him order me around again. It's time Hugh stopped taking everything for granted—especially me!"

She pressed a shaking hand to her temple. "I think I could use those aspirin now, Chad."

After watching while she swallowed the pills and thirstily finished the rest of the water, Chad took the empty glass and set it on the counter. "A hot relaxing bath and then bed is what you need, little witch."

Casey just knew the hair was standing straight up on her head. Avoiding his eyes, she headed toward the back door on wobbly legs. As she opened her mouth to speak, she prayed her voice wouldn't squeak with nervousness. "Thank you for your help tonight."

With one hand she flipped the release latch on the sliding door. She consciously wiped her face free of emotion when she turned to usher him out. To her stupefaction all she got for her polite effort was a terrific view of his back. Noticing the way the material of his shirt fit across his wide shoulders, she couldn't help wondering if he had his clothes specially made for him.

"Hurry up, Casey."

With a start of surprise she realized that Chad had halted and was now turned impatiently in her direction. She looked from him to the stairs, and then back again. "The sooner you leave," she said, lending special emphasis to the last word, "the sooner I can lock up and get to bed."

Chad simply shook his head in a negative gesture. "If that little conversation I overheard was as upsetting as it seemed, you'll spend most of the night tossing and turning if you don't unwind first. Anyway, a long soak in a hot tub of water will help ease the soreness in your back."

She sighed with barely controlled impatience. "Then I'll take a bath if it'll make you happy," she muttered, her mouth thinning as she gestured toward the door. "You can leave with your mind at rest."

"I'm not leaving you alone until you're through with your bath."

"I've been bathing myself for quite a few years, Chad."

"Not after taking medication," he said, his expression stern.

She gritted her teeth at his stubbornness. "Then I won't take a bath!"

"The hell you won't," he remarked cheerfully, turning and beginning to take the stairs two at a time. "Now behave yourself and don't argue."

"I told you, I never argue!"

Since he was already out of sight, she had to yell to make herself heard. Tilting her head in a listening attitude, she waited, and when no sound emerged from upstairs she angrily slid the lock on the door back into place.

"Stubborn, pig-headed jackass," she mumbled, switching off the lights as she stomped toward the foot of the stairs. Other, stronger epithets were tumbling about in her mind as she began to climb, and she could hardly wait to blister Chad's ears with them.

6

~~~~~~~~~~~~

Casey reached the bathroom in record time and found Chad bent over her shiny white enamel bathtub. She was ready to explode with frustration at his arbitrary behavior. He seemed to think he could simply walk into her house and take over, she thought indignantly. God alone knew how tired she was of dominating males who never questioned anyone's wishes but their own!

She opened her mouth to translate her anger into words, but no sound emerged. The look of studied concentration on his face as he sprinkled violet-scented bath crystals into the steaming water sent a wave of tenderness through her. How many times had she seen that same expression on her son's face when he wanted to please her by performing some unfamiliar task? His brow would furrow into a downward curve above the bridge of his nose, just as Chad's was doing now.

Her breathing slowed as the anger she'd felt minutes before dispersed as quickly as the frothy bubbles in the tub. She inhaled the sweet, steam-dampened air with almost as much pleasure as she viewed the full thrust of Chad's lower lip. A gentle light glowed in her eyes as she noticed the recalcitrant lock of hair that lay over his forehead. He looked so much like a little boy trying to please teacher, she thought. When he straightened and turned to face her, she was almost startled to see him holding a box of bath crystals instead of an apple.

"Did I put too much in?"

At the distracted note in his voice she smiled and glanced at the bubbles nearly overflowing the edge of the tub. "Thank you, it looks lovely."

She was fascinated by the color that surged into his cheeks at her praise, but another quick glance at the rising water level convinced her to think in terms of practicalities. "Umm, don't you think you'd better turn it off now?"

Chad closed the faucets with an acknowledging grunt, his expression sheepish as he handed her a large bath towel. At that moment she wanted nothing so much as to hug him. Made uneasy by the thought, she started to turn away. "I'll just get my robe."

Instantly she found her hand being clasped as Chad pulled her through the doorway and into the room. "Just tell me where it is and I'll get it for you."

Casey hesitated, but the eager light in his eyes overcame her reluctance. He was enthusiastically determined to take care of her needs, and a hidden part of her reveled in the attention she was receiving from him. During her childhood, she had been treated as one of the boys, and later it was she who ministered to the needs of her father and brothers. She had never in her life been waited on, and she found the experience to be delightfully pleasurable.

Chad, she realized, made her feel like a delicate flower being coaxed into unfurling her petals to embrace the warmth of the sun. Even while she told him where her robe could be found, her mind was already grappling with the implications of her thoughts. Was she in danger of thinking of Chad as necessary to her happiness?

The idea of emotional dependence was frightening. She didn't want to return to being a doormat for another egocentric male. She didn't want to be seduced into acting out a role for which she was ill-suited. Yet by the intensity of her inner response to Chad, she suspected that the independence she prized so highly was being threatened. Instinctively she sensed that once she fell under the influence of Chad's personality, she would lose even the small part of herself she had been able to withhold from Hugh.

Her husband had attempted to force her submission through physical as well as mental subjugation. He had nearly succeeded, she remembered with a twinge of disgust. But even in the short time she'd known Chad, she suspected that he would never have to resort to force to gain his objectives. He was strong, and his strength would be a lure to any woman. To her horror she recognized a deep-seated feminine longing to lean on him, and instantly rejected its presence. It was a sign of weakness, one she couldn't afford. She wouldn't allow herself to become emotionally dependent on Chad because she knew she couldn't cope with the results of such dependency.

She sighed and glanced despondently at her reflection in the mirror above the washbasin. Green eyes looked back at her, their depths shadowed by her thoughts. She viewed those shadows dispassionately, her mouth firming in resistance to the evidence of her own vulnerability. She heard Chad's footsteps in the hallway with a feeling of relief. She needed to be distracted from the unpleasantness of her memories, and as he appeared in the open doorway with her robe clutched in his hand she found herself studying him with more than casual interest.

If she was honest with herself, she thought suddenly, she would have to accept the fact that where Chad was concerned, her interest had never been casual. From the beginning he had arrested her attention. She had felt a moment of instant recognition, as if she and Chad were two halves of one whole, or two souls permanently joined together throughout eternity. A long time ago she had been romantic enough to want to believe in the idea that there was just one man for each woman. Since Chad had entered her life, this ideology was beginning to appear more and more plausible.

It was a dangerous philosophy, she realized with a tremor of fear. To become dependent on someone else for her happiness would leave her vulnerable and open to manipulation the way she'd been in her marriage. And it would be so much worse with Chad. Hugh had never fulfilled her basic needs, but she knew that Chad would not be satisfied with less than full physical and emotional surrender. She had a sneaking suspicion that it wasn't in him to settle for anything but total commitment.

She realized with shuddering anguish that when Hugh had tired of her, her pain had been mixed with relief. Instead of pandering to a masculine ego that needed constant reassurance, she had been left to become her own person, an individual in her own right. But to allow Chad into her life would be to risk all she had accomplished, because even now the emotions he inspired in her made what she had once felt for Hugh a pale shadow in comparison.

"What's wrong, Casey?"

The question was a terse whisper, and yet it penetrated her preoccupation with the immediacy of cannon fire. She blinked, and then focused on the concern in Chad's expression. His eyes roamed her face as though searching for an answer. She sensed his struggle to see through the barriers she had placed between them after Hugh's call. She should have been reassured by his perception;

instead she was upset. With a feeling of extreme sadness she realized that Hugh, unlike Chad, had never wanted to see past his own image of her.

To him she had simply been an extension of himself. That realization brought hitherto unasked questions to her mind. Had Hugh's selfishness in their relationship kept her from being a wife in the truest sense of the word? *Was* she inept as a woman, as he had so often claimed? Or had Chad guessed the truth? Could it have been Hugh's failure to live up to what *she* had expected of *him* that had brought about the destruction of their marriage? The questions revolved uselessly in her mind. If I let Chad make love to me, an inner voice whispered seductively, would at least one of those questions be answered? The thought shocked her, and she could feel the color drain from her face.

"Casey, what is it? Tell me what's wrong."

She inhaled a steadying breath and forced a reassuring smile to her lips. "Nothing's wrong, Chad. I guess I'm just tired."

"Are you sure?" The hands he lifted to her shoulders were more than a little demanding.

Her voice was tinged with impatience when she said, "No matter what you think to the contrary, I do know my own mind."

"Then why the shadow in your eyes, Katherine? For a moment you looked almost haunted."

This man sees entirely too much, she thought. "All your effort will be wasted if I don't get into that bath. I've never been partial to washing in cold water."

Her ploy worked, and although his eyes still held a lingering doubt he released her shoulders and walked toward the doorway. "Would you like a cup of hot chocolate?"

"I'd rather have coffee."

He shook his head. "Coffee's much too stimulating. Chocolate will help you sleep."

"Yes, Daddy," she mocked.

The door was closing behind him, but at her words his head reappeared in the opening. "The yes was perfect, but I would pay better attention if you called me darling."

The towel she still held in her hand sailed through the air in his direction. The impulse served to lighten her spirits, and she found herself smiling with satisfaction. But before the soft folds could connect with his laughing face, he ducked out of the line of fire, and slammed the door closed behind him. Still grinning, Casey stared down at the crumpled towel on the floor before retrieving it and draping it over the towel rack with exaggerated care. She'd darling him, she thought, chuckling softly as she began to dispense with her clothing. He was a rude, managing, bossy . . .

The temperature was just right, she decided, stepping into the water and maneuvering her body until she lay with her head against the rim. Closing her eyes, she stretched her legs out until her toes connected with the opposite end of the tub, and thought of new adjectives to describe Chad. She was still irritated with him for refusing to leave before she'd finished her bath, but the sharpness of her anger was fading with the relaxation of both her mind and body.

By the time he made it back to his motel it was going to be very late, she thought with a twinge of compunction, and he was going to feel like hell tomorrow. When he'd driven her home from the chiropractor's office, Chad had discussed the union demands that were causing him so much worry. She had listened to words like "available cash flow," "long-term pension investments," and "budget cuts" with growing respect. She was made to see the difference between Hugh's idea of the role of a business executive and Chad's. Hugh's only concern was self-advancement and public image. But Chad was terribly concerned for the employees who would suffer a layoff if the demands of the union rose beyond funds readily available to his firm. Given time, he had explained, the drain on company resources caused by the opening of the Bay Area subsidiary would be alleviated as the new plant gained in productivity.

"But what happens if the union representatives press their claims, Chad?" she had asked.

His expression was grim as he replied, "That's what I'm afraid of, honey. They'll probably strike, and the loss in productivity will only hamper our ability to negotiate. A lot of families will be hurt financially by the delay. The thought of such senseless waste makes my blood boil."

"Isn't there any way you can convince them you need more time?"

He shrugged, his hands tightening around the

steering wheel as he entered the condominium complex. "There's an instinctive distrust between management and union, but I'm hoping I made a favorable impression today. We were at it until nearly six o'clock, and I barely made my plane on time."

He drove into one of the visitor parking spaces and killed the engine before turning to smile at her. "Now do you forgive me for neglecting to call you?"

"Yes, but I'm furious with you for neglecting your health. Why in the world didn't you stay in Los Angeles tonight?" she demanded, her eyes eloquent with disapproval.

"Because the union representatives are spending the next few days coming to a decision, and whichever way the ball bounces, I'm going to have to return to our L.A. office as soon as I hear from them. I wanted to spend as much time as possible with you and Jonathan before I was summoned back."

Remembering his words, the last vestiges of Casey's anger fled. She arched her back in the water, comforted by the knowledge that Chad had missed her company as much as she had missed his. But even though it was pleasant to be shown so much care and attention, she found herself wishing he hadn't bothered tonight. He was probably the one who needed to rest, and even after taking those muscle relaxants she wasn't at all sleepy. She yawned deeply, her eyes closing as she luxuriated in the peace of her surroundings. . . .

Casey didn't know whether it was the cooler air from the hallway that awakened her, or the firm hand that cupped the back of her neck and lifted her into a sitting position. Before she had a chance to decide, another hand slipped under her knees, and she was being lifted out of the water. A moment later she found herself sharing the bathmat with a decidedly masculine pair of feet. Somehow, as the mists of sleep cleared from her mind, she found that the sight of Chad's stocking feet made her more self-conscious than her own nakedness.

"What do y . . . you think you're d . . . doing?"

His chest shook with restrained laughter. "I'm drying you off."

She wriggled against the arms that held her, her hands bunched into helpless fists at her sides. "Haven't you ever heard of a person's right to privacy?"

"I gave you half an hour of privacy," he remarked, briskly rubbing the towel over her body before stepping back to wrap her in its damp folds. "When I knocked and you didn't answer, it scared the hell out of me. How was I to know when I hurried to the rescue that I'd find a snoring mermaid instead of a drowned witch?"

"I wasn't snoring!"

He smiled cryptically and refused to respond to her indignant exclamation. His studied silence shook her composure. Timidly she asked, "Was I?"

"Were you what?" He grinned, and tightened his grip on the ends of the towel.

"Snoring!"

With a frustrated grimace she brushed aside the hands that rested beneath her throat. She was so busy concentrating on his expressive features she didn't realize that the tucked ends of the towel had parted until the damp terry cloth began sliding toward the floor. She froze in embarrassment.

As though unconscious of making any movement, he lifted his hands slowly, his gaze smoldering as the tips of her small breasts puckered beneath the heat of his perusal. Shocked into immobility by the desire surging so unexpectedly between them, Casey felt helpless to halt the inevitability of his next move. As she watched, the ends of his fingers brushed against her hardened nipples before lowering to span her waist. Her mind screamed at her to retreat, but she couldn't seem to make her body obey. With one featherlight touch he had created a craving deep inside her, and as he pulled her toward the tightening thrust of his hard body she stepped forward blindly.

"Your body is perfect," he breathed, his glance smoldering with repressed fire as her breasts touched his chest.

Her eyes widened in wonder as she registered the sincerity in his rasping tones. Hugh had often teased her about her boyish shape, and she winced as she remembered the pain his ridicule had caused her. It was only now, as she viewed the admiration in Chad's eyes, that she realized how much her self-image had suffered because of her husband's callousness. Her expressive face must have registered the remembered hurt, because Chad immediately showed his concern. He loosened his hold and reached for her robe, his mouth grim as he helped her put it on.

"God, I really pick my times," he muttered in disgust. "Your back's probably aching like the devil, and I'm standing here gawking at you. Let's get you into bed before you faint."

"I'm not in any pain," she mumbled, and felt heat scorch her cheeks when she realized how much that sounded like an invitation.

But Chad only averted his eyes from her bewildered features as he led her out of the bathroom. The arm he placed around her waist had become an impersonal tool used to guide her direction. The passion had been wiped from his expression. Casey, however, found she couldn't turn her emotions off so quickly. Her body still vibrated with the depth of the response he had unsuspectingly wrung from her, and as they entered her bedroom her emotions swung like a pendulum from elation to embarrassed confusion.

As if to give her time to compose herself, Chad left her side to turn down the covers on the bed. The light from the bedside lamp turned his hair to gold and cast shadows over his stern features. He looked disturbed, and she knew his mood had been caused by that scene in the bathroom. Oh, God! As if their relationship wasn't strained enough, she had to fall asleep in the tub and complicate matters. At the thought, she crossed her arms over her chest and gripped her elbows with trembling hands.

She saw her bare pink toes peeping from beneath the hem of her robe, and tried to hide them within the deep pile of the carpet. She still felt as exposed as any centerfold pinup. The memory of Chad's eyes roaming over what her robe now covered was enough to keep the feeling alive, and she dreaded the moment when she would have to meet his eyes.

"Aren't you going to drink your chocolate?"

The question was so prosaic; Casey's eyes left her inspection of the carpet and went to Chad's gesticulating hand. There on the nightstand was a cup with a slight wisp of steam rising from its contents. The last thing she wanted was a hot drink, but she welcomed the opportunity to perform a familiar task. Maybe then Chad would leave, she thought hopefully, and she would be able to come to terms with the agonizing shyness she felt when she looked at him.

She avoided his eyes as she sat on the edge of the bed and lifted the cup to her lips. The too sweet taste made her stomach contract protestingly, but not by the flicker of an eyelash did she reveal her revulsion. She wanted to finish it as quickly as possible and then hide herself under her covers for the rest of the night. As for Chad, her only defense against the way he was making her feel was trying to pretend he didn't exist.

But pretense was one thing and reality another. How could you shut a man's existence out of your consciousness when he stood directly in front of you and quietly began cursing as he deprived you of your unwanted drink? How could you ignore his presence when he sat beside you and drew you against the warmth of his body? How could you convince yourself he was a figment of your imagination when he pressed you down onto a soft mattress and covered you with his demanding weight?

Casey discovered forgetfulness was impossible when Chad's gentle mouth closed her eyes with kisses and then shifted to drink deeply of her parted lips. She knew she wasn't either mentally or emotionally prepared for what was happening, and yet her body seemed to be reacting to the stimulus Chad provided whether she wanted it to or not. The warm mouth wandering across her face was first soft with persuasion, then hard with fierce insistence. The hand that moved against her neck and shoulders was gentled by tenderness, yet heavy with barely leashed possessiveness. She was being made love to by a man of contrasts and she was unable to resist him. Hard, soft, gentle, fierce . . . he was all of them.

Her arms lifted to twine themselves around his neck, and she knew she wanted him with a desperation that left her helpless in his hands. She was powerless against his sweet brand of persuasion. She could lie to herself from now until doomsday, she thought dizzily, without altering that most basic of truths.

"Katherine?"

Her head moved restlessly against the tangled bedclothes. She didn't want to talk . . . didn't want words to shatter her concentration. She needed to lose herself in Chad without answering the questions that hovered in the back of her mind. With uncharacteristic aggression she buried her fingers in his hair and drew his mouth down to hers.

Her lips opened to feed his hunger and her own. She could feel Chad tense in her arms and knew he was trying to refrain from fully releasing his passion. But she didn't want to be guided and coaxed and pacified like a child. She wanted to be convinced; to know beyond any shadow of a doubt that she was wanted. Please, Chad, she cried silently, her body twisting restlessly against him. Please stop me from thinking and teach me to feel.

She was oblivious to the sound of her own moans until she heard him speak. "It's all right, Casey," he said, his arms tightening convulsively as he rested his damp forehead against her shoulder. "I'm not going to hurt you, love. Please . . . don't cry."

It was then that she felt the betraying moisture trickling from the corners of her eyes. Her lashes lifted, and she viewed his remorse with anguish. He was lifting himself from her, and she began to shake as his warmth was withdrawn. "No . . . oh, no," she groaned, losing her last contact with him when her hands slid from around his neck.

He shook his head, his eyes dark with leashed desire. "You're not ready for this."

"I am, I . . ."

He placed the pad of his thumb against her lower

lip and rubbed gently. "I won't be used, Katherine."

Her eyes widened, and they were filled with flashing anger. "I'm not using you!"

"Then why goad me into losing control?"

"How dare you suggest that I . . . ?"

"Oh, I'll dare almost anything to have you," he muttered, pushing himself into a sitting position. He braced his hands on either side of her head and leaned forward to search her eyes. "But I will not resort to taking my pleasure at your expense."

Her low tones were barely distinguishable, and yet they held a bitterness she couldn't deny. "Why don't you just tell me I turned you off, and get out of here? I can assure you I'm well able to handle that kind of rejection. I've certainly had enough practice!"

"You little fool," he uttered harshly, grabbing her hand and guiding it to the juncture of his thighs. "Does this feel like I'm turned off?"

Her fingers momentarily flexed in fascinated curiosity, and just as abruptly withdrew. "All right, then I was the one who was turned off."

The sarcastic inflection in her voice wiped all traces of restraint from his expression. With a low growl of anger he reached for her robe and yanked the loose folds apart. "Like hell you were!"

Before she could avert her eyes Chad's head descended, and as she watched, his tongue rubbed hungrily against one hardened nipple. Her arms stiffened at her sides and she bunched the crumpled sheet in her hands until her fingers cramped painfully.

She wanted to arch against his mouth, and it took the last vestiges of her strength to deny the impulse. "I think I've been suitably punished, Chad." With a strangled cry she released her hold on the bedclothes and pushed at his shoulders. "Now you can leave with your ego intact."

His mouth slid to her throat, and she felt the warm expulsion of his breath against her skin with a shiver of lingering desire. "Oh, Casey! Is that what you think this is all about?" he questioned tiredly.

"What else am I supposed to think?"

Slowly he lifted himself until he stood beside the bed, and before she could protest he grabbed her hands and pulled her to her feet. With a casual nonchalance she envied, he straightened her gaping robe and tied the belt firmly at her waist. Then he placed his hands on her shoulders and drew her close to his warmth.

"I know you won't believe this, but I'm showing my love for you in the only way possible. I'm too much a hedonist to advocate self-denial, but with you there doesn't seem to be much alternative, Katherine.

"A little while ago on that bed," he said, pointing at it, "you were urging me to take all responsibility for our actions. If I'd made love to you, and God alone knows how badly I want to love you, we would have enjoyed a satisfying experience without any commitment. Don't you think I could see how much that call from Hugh upset you tonight? But I won't be used as a means to drive those shadows from your eyes, Katherine. I want more from you than you're ready to give me, and whether you know it or not, you have the right to demand more from me. When we share our bodies it's going to be because you need me in every way there is to need a man. I don't ever want to wake up with you in my arms, only to find you haven't let me into your heart."

He left with the quiet tread characteristic of the man, and Casey watched his departure with burning eyes and a regret that left her aching to call him back. But the cry remained locked in her throat, accompanied by the lump of emotion her tears couldn't dispel. She could say the words he wanted to hear, she thought. Soft, gentle words of love, and need, and want. But she wasn't certain she was ready to have him believe them. As she stared at the empty doorway she wondered if she would ever be prepared to believe them herself.

7

Casey twisted restlessly in the lounger, watching as Jonathan splashed happily at the shallow end of their clubhouse pool. The late August sunshine spread warmth over her bikini-clad body as she listened to the excited squeals of her son and his playmates, and she found herself envying them their uncomplicated enjoyment of the bright summer day. Ever since Hugh had returned to San Ramon a month earlier, she had been plagued by a sense of uneasiness. A feeling of homesickness overwhelmed her as she recalled the hot, golden summers of her own childhood in southern California, and she longed to recapture the security of those long-ago days.

"Mmmm, you're turning a nice toasty color."

With a gasp Casey sat up and looked into her

ex-husband's face. It was a pleasant face, she thought, with an impartiality that amazed her, considering they'd been married four years and divorced for less than two. He had brown hair, brown eyes, and pale skin that spoke of hours spent behind a desk. She noted that his thin, though well-proportioned, body was as immaculately clad as ever in tan slacks and a cream and gold sport shirt, wondering if he was hoping to impress her with the predictable tastefulness of his attire. A vivid image of Chad tussling with Jonathan at the park entered her mind, his chest bare above a pair of ragged cutoffs. She couldn't begin to imagine Hugh compromising his dignity in such a manner, she thought derisively.

"You startled me," she said, her expression distant. "What are you doing here?"

"So welcoming," he responded, hitching up his pants to preserve their crease as he seated himself on the end of the lounger. "But you haven't exactly been a model of good cheer since I've been back, have you, Casey?"

"I've allowed you to visit with Jonathan whenever you wanted, not that you've asked to have him very often."

His mouth hardened, his eyes accusing as they wandered suggestively over her body. "I wasn't exactly pleased to find you both helping Walker move in next door the last time I came to pick Jonathan up. Why should I make it easy for you to spend time alone with your . . . neighbor?"

"I don't need you to aid in my leisure pursuits,

Hugh. Unlike you, Chad enjoys Jonathan's company."

"That smacks of criticism, my love."

"You're damn right it does!"

She jerked her foot away when he reached out to caress her ankle. From the moment Hugh had shown up at her door a month ago, he had done his best to insinuate himself back into her life. What she hated most was the way he used Jonathan to accomplish his aim. He had begun his campaign by paying marked attention to his son, but that hadn't lasted long. When she consistently refused to accompany them on any of their outings, he had quickly reverted to character, and Jonathan was more often than not ignored by his father.

"Have dinner with me tonight, Casey."

She had turned her attention to her son, her eyes eloquent with pride as she watched the sturdy young arms in bright blue inflatable floats practicing the swimming strokes Chad had taught him. But at the insistence in Hugh's voice, she nervously turned to face her ex-husband. The avidity of his gaze quite literally turned her stomach, and she reached for her robe before attempting to reply to his invitation. She saw the angry flush that mottled his cheekbones as she hid herself from his heated perusal, and noticed the cruelty in his thin-lipped mouth as he stared at her. There was jealousy in those eyes, and malevolence, and a sickening possessiveness.

Trembling, she avoided a direct answer. "Jonathan has to be up early tomorrow for nursery school."

"I don't remember inviting Jonathan," he replied with sarcasm, leaning forward to trail a finger down her cheek. "Sally can watch the boy while you and I have dinner at my apartment. We haven't had a chance to be alone, and we've got a lot to talk about."

She flinched from his touch and surveyed him with antagonism. "You're very free with Sally's time. That's rather hypocritical when you've made your dislike of her so obvious, isn't it?"

"She's an interfering old busybody!"

"She can't help being protective of Jonathan, Hugh. She and Bill have been like grandparents to him. You should be kinder to them for Jonathan's sake."

"Why should I bother?" he exclaimed angrily. "They're nothing to me . . . or to my son."

"That's where you're wrong," she retorted, her eyes sparkling dangerously. "Your rude behavior toward two people he loves is hurtful and confusing to Jonathan. He wants to look up to you, but you're not giving him much of an example to follow, are you? If only you'd stop trying to intimidate me by using a defenseless child, you might begin to see Jonathan as an individual instead of some kind of living link to the past."

"Quit using the boy as a shield to hide behind, Casey. It's you and I we should be talking about!"

"We have nothing to say to each other, Hugh."

Getting to his feet, Hugh pushed his hands into the pockets of his slacks. His stance was meant to be intimidating, and she was comforted by her lack of reaction. A long time ago a younger, more easily influenced Casey had been cowed by his manner, she remembered. But she was no longer the innocent fool she had been, content to bask in the big man's shadow. She was an individual in her own right, and she was not about to be daunted by Hugh's belligerent attitude.

To a large degree, she had Chad to thank for her self-confidence, she realized. He had proven himself a rock on whom she could lean, and the only person who truly understood the problems she was facing with Jonathan. Contrary to what Hugh believed, since that night when Chad had walked away from her bed he had kept their relationship platonic. He had moved into the unit next door shortly after Hugh's arrival in town, and made it clear he was there if she needed him. He acted as if nothing had happened to alter their relationship, but she knew that wasn't true. There was now a reticence in his manner when he looked at her along with the affection in his eyes, and his wariness hurt her more than she wanted to admit.

If only, she thought frantically, she could find a way to escape from Hugh's constant harassment. She'd tried being rational but had failed to get her feelings across to him. His image of her is fixed in his mind, and no matter how often she showed her independence, he still viewed her as some clinging female in need of male guidance. When his blandishments had failed to bring about the desired results, he'd shown up at her door late one evening and tried brute force.

At least she'd had the presence of mind to phone Chad before letting Hugh inside, she remembered, with a cold knot of tension forming in her stomach. After the most perfunctory of greetings Hugh had begun a physical assault that still made her shudder at the recollection. If he hadn't been interrupted by Chad's entry, she knew that Hugh would have enforced his imagined claim to her in the most disgusting manner possible.

After Hugh had stormed out of the house, his eyes flashing hatred for them both, she had confessed as much to Chad. He had studied her distraught features silently, his mouth grim in the gray pallor of his face. "God, you shouldn't have stopped me from slamming my fist into his gut. When I walked in here and saw you struggling with him, I wanted to kill the bastard!"

"Violence wouldn't have solved anything, Chad."

"Maybe not," he agreed, lingering rage still evident in his expression. His gaze studied the white lines of tension bracketing her mouth, and he seemed to struggle inwardly to display a calmness he was far from feeling. "He wants you, Katherine."

She nodded, her fists clenched at her sides. "I found that out tonight." Half-hysterical laughter burst from her throat. "It's quite a change from our married days, when Hugh found me the least appealing of his female acquaintances. There must be some truth behind the saying that forbidden fruit tastes sweeter."

"And what do you want, Casey?" he asked quietly.

Her expression conveyed a plea for understanding as she whispered, "Did I look like I was encouraging him, Chad?"

"Appearances can be deceiving," he said, his mouth twisting cynically. "You could be subconsciously punishing him for his earlier treatment of you."

"If that was true, could you blame me?"

He shook his head, but then he whispered, "Please . . . don't hate him, Casey."

Confused, she simply stared at him. "You mean you wouldn't care if Hugh and I . . . ?"

With a low groan of anguish he slammed his fist into the wall, and half turned away from her. "You don't know me at all if you think I don't care. It's tearing me apart to see the hold that swine has over you, especially since I know how close hate can be to love. You're losing weight and if those circles under your eyes are any indication, you haven't been sleeping all that well. But you won't give me the right to put an end to it. Hugh's not the only one you're keeping at a distance, Katherine."

"You don't understand," she cried, "and it's not fair of you to make such a comparison. I have to try to solve my problems in my own way, Chad. Not so long ago you told me you wouldn't be used, and

I've tried to respect your wishes. Maybe I shouldn't have called you tonight, but I was reacting to a situation I couldn't handle alone."

His features gentled as he absorbed her distress. "I'm not talking about what happened tonight." His jaw clenched briefly before he continued. "We both know what would have happened if I hadn't arrived."

"Then what *are* you talking about?"

"I'm trying to get you to see your confusion logically and to come to terms with what you really want from our relationship."

"I don't know what I want any longer. All I'm certain of at the moment are my feelings toward Hugh."

Chad's mouth twisted. "Are you saying you might still love him, Casey?"

"Do you take me for a fool?"

"Not a fool," he said succinctly, his mouth drawing down at the corners, "but a woman filled with too much pride to accept a logical solution to her problems."

"Because of Hugh's obstinacy there's nothing logical about this situation."

"There's a sure way to convince him it's over between you."

She gazed at him warily, her distress increasing at the implacable expression in his eyes. "Short of entering a nunnery, I don't see how that would be possible."

"You could marry me," he murmured gently.

"The old marriage of convenience?"

"You know I want you, and you're not naive enough to believe I wouldn't make it a true marriage in every respect."

His statement was uttered without a shred of emotion, as though he were proposing a business merger. Oh, yes, she thought bitterly. She knew he wanted her, but she also knew that physical desire alone wasn't enough. She needed to be viewed as an equal, and his protectiveness now was insulting. If he wasn't afraid she was capable of giving in to Hugh's pressuring, she reasoned, he wouldn't feel he had to stake his own claim.

"I'm sick to death of hearing what Hugh wants, so don't you start in on me, Chad," she muttered furiously. "I appreciate your offer, but contrary to what you and my ex-husband believe, I don't need a man to lean on. I went into one marriage with my eyes closed, and I don't intend to make the same mistake twice. You're offering to marry me in good faith, and I do appreciate the sacrifice. But I value your friendship too much to take you up on it. Call it pride, or good, old-fashioned morals. Either way, I refuse to view marriage as a way out of a dilemma. Believe me, I've learned that particular lesson the hard way."

"Then if you're in full control of your own life, why haven't you sent that idiot about his business? Instead of calling me tonight, why didn't you phone the police and have them issue a restraining order?"

She flinched at the accusation in his voice, then shook her head tiredly. "Because Jonathan *is* Hugh's business, and I have no right to deprive my son of his father!"

"Yes, biologically Hugh is Jonathan's father," he said, "but in every other way he's waived his right to the title, Katherine. Most young, sexually active men are capable of creating a child, but it takes more than an act of nature to make them a father. I should know," he concluded harshly. "My own father walked out on my mother and me when I was little older than Jon. Like you, she had to struggle to support us both."

Casey gasped, her eyes wide as she saw the bitterness of the past on his face. "I'm sorry."

"Don't be," he said shortly, running his hand across the back of his neck in a curiously vulnerable gesture. "When I was twelve my mother married again, and she's found the happiness she deserved to have in the first place. He's a good man, my stepfather. At that age I was jealous and resentful, and I'm afraid I made his life hell for quite a while. God alone knows why, but he persevered in his attempts to reach me. Then one day he came home from work, and I watched as he put his arms around my mother. I wanted to shout at him to keep his hands to himself, and I know my face showed all the hate I was feeling in that instant."

Chad cleared his throat and shook his head ruefully. "I'll never forget the pain in his eyes when he looked at me. He didn't reproach me for my belligerence, just smiled gently, and said, 'Hello, son.' That was how I learned that hate and love can intertwine, until we no longer know what we really feel, Casey. Henry loved my mother, but he loved me as well. It was then I knew I returned that love."

"Did your real father ever visit you?"

To Casey's dismay, Chad's hands closed angrily over her shoulders. "Haven't you been listening to a thing I've been saying?" His face was dark with frustration as his fingers tightened on the soft flesh of her upper arms.

"It was only a figure of speech," she cried, twisting to relieve the pressure of his hold.

"You want to talk about 'real' fathers, Katherine? All right, I'll give you my definition. A 'real' father doesn't discard his son along with his wife, like an unwanted piece of garbage. Nor does he use his child to gain his own ends. He's loving and caring, but most of all . . . he's there to guide a young boy into manhood. The man who helped my mother conceive me was no more my father than Hugh is Jonathan's. It was Henry Walker who took on that responsibility, and it's Henry Walker who deserves the credit."

Her mouth softened with compassion. "You took your stepfather's name?"

Now Chad's hands loosened, and his thumbs began to smooth away the pain caused by his convulsive grasp. "Not at first," he admitted, his tone distracted. "I was christened Charles Murray, after my father. To avoid confusion my mother began calling me Chad." He grinned. "She couldn't stand the thought of having me referred to as Charlie. A wise woman, my mother."

She responded to his smile, but there was still curiosity in her gaze. "It's natural that you would have returned your stepfather's affection. A child has a great capacity for love, and the love you feel for your stepfather in no way diminishes the relationship you might have had with your r . . . with your father," she amended hastily.

His laughter was abrupt and uneven. "You're wrong, Casey. Until my father put in a belated appearance I had no means of comparing him to Henry. I used to wonder if I felt the same about Henry as my friends did about their fathers, and as I got older my doubts placed a strain on our relationship. But when I was sixteen Charles Murray showed up at our door, trying to foster feelings in me that simply didn't exist. Although it distressed my mother when I agreed to spend some time with him, Henry knew I needed to satisfy my curiosity about the man who'd given me life. I returned home two days later and found my stepfather closeted in his den. He asked no questions, Casey. He took one look at my face and simply held his arms out to me. Later we talked, and it was then I realized that the bitterness I'd felt toward my father was gone. All I felt was pity, because of the indifference I felt for him. That was when I asked Henry if I could legally take his name as my own."

"You saw yourself in Jonathan from the beginning, didn't you, Chad?" Even as she whispered the words, she saw the answer in his eyes.

"That's why I'm afraid for him, Casey," he muttered hoarsely, drawing her forward until her head rested on his chest. "For you both. Hugh waves his paternity like a banner, but from what I can see I don't think he feels anything for Jon. He's using the boy to get at you, and you're letting him get away with it."

"What do you expect me to do?" she cried, tilting her head back until his face came into view. "Jonathan's only four years old, not sixteen and nearly grown, Chad. I don't have the right to influence his decisions. There's still time for him to establish a relationship with Hugh. I have to consider Jon's welfare, can't you understand that? I can tell Hugh we're through, but legally and morally I'm forced to welcome him when he visits his son."

"And have you?"

"Have I what?"

His arms tightened, and a look of anguish deepened the new lines of worry in his face. "Have you told him you're through?"

She felt a need to hide from the intensity of his expression, and lowered her eyes. "In a roundabout way," she admitted. "I haven't wanted to antagonize him, for Jonathan's sake."

She saw Chad's chest expand as he drew a rasping breath, and his arms fell away from her. It was then that he suggested he return to Los Angeles.

She'd stared at him incredulously. "But you've ironed out the difficulties with the union. After they agreed to give you the time you asked for, you told me you wouldn't have to go back for a while."

He avoided her eyes. "You need some space, Katherine."

"I don't, I need . . ."

His hand slashed the air in a violent gesture. "Please . . . don't put any more temptation in my path."

He turned away, his shoulders slumped in momentary defeat. "I'm not exactly impartial in this situation, Casey. I have my own wants and needs, and they quite effectively bias my opinion of your ex-husband's motives. And though you might deny it, you're being influenced by my attitude. I already know what I want, but you're confused and uncertain."

"I may have a lot on my mind, but I'm not stupid, Chad." She drew closer to his side and touched his arm. "I don't want Hugh!"

The memory of the words she'd spoken to Chad over a week ago were still resounding in her head, and as she listened to Hugh insisting that they talk out their problems for Jonathan's sake she was gripped with anger. Chad had been right to doubt her decisiveness, she thought in disgust. But the time had come to set Hugh straight on a few points. She'd delayed the inevitable confrontation long enough.

Her voice was scathing as she faced her ex-husband. "Oh, come off it, Hugh! Do you really expect me to believe this sudden concern for Jonathan's future when it's taken you nearly two years to develop a father instinct?"

"I sent my child support!"

"Sporadically, yes."

He looked at first shamefaced, then defiant. "I had other obligations to meet."

"I'm not disputing your priorities, Hugh," she said tightly. "But Jonathan should be more to you than an obligation."

"I don't see what chance there is of that," he snapped, his eyes narrowing with scorn. "All the kid talks about when he's with me is his friend Chad."

"For God's sake, what did you expect? Jonathan wasn't even three years old when you left, and you weren't overly concerned at the time about the effect your leaving might have on him."

"Tell me something, Casey," he said, observing her through narrowed eyes. "Am I right in suspecting this Chad character is Mommy's friend, as well as Jonathan's? Or is 'friend' the right word?"

She stiffened with indignation. "What business is it of yours?"

"He's your playmate, too, isn't he, Casey?" he demanded, his features twisting into an ugly mask. "Isn't that why you're on the defensive?"

"You have no right to question my relationships."

"Who has a better right?" he demanded, managing to look as pompous as he sounded. "Jonathan deserves to have both his parents. He needs his father, not some handy facsimile."

Casey rose hurriedly, unable to believe what she was hearing. She was appalled by Hugh's air of smug satisfaction, and for the first time she realized what a closed-minded, opinionated man he had become beneath his surface urbanity. "Unlike you," she said coldly, "Chad isn't trying to play a role. He loves Jonathan, and the feeling is reciprocated."

"Damn you, quit trying to pull the wool over my eyes. I've seen the way he looks at you, Casey. It's disgusting!"

She controlled the shakiness of her voice by breathing deeply, her heightened emotions noticeable only in the hands tensed at her sides. "Wasn't it disgusting when you were romancing the boss's daughter?"

"I made a mistake."

He admitted it with less concern than he would show over discovering a piece of lint clinging to his carefully creased slacks. As he waited for her reaction, his expression indicated egotistical self-confidence. "Susan meant nothing to me, Casey. I never should have left you and Jonathan for her. But I'll make it up to you. After we're married again, I'll . . ."

Her breath issued explosively from her lungs. How could he find justification for his own infidelity so easily and in the same conversation attack her morals? "You presumptuous bastard!"

"All right, so we've both made mistakes," he

admitted, his eyes shifting uneasily. "I had an affair with Susan, and you've been sleeping with Walker. The score is even, but I still hold the advantage."

Her mouth twisted in disgust. "Just how do you figure that one?"

"Walker isn't Jonathan's father, I am. And I'm ready to resume my responsibilities to both of you. What more do you want?"

What more did she want? No real concern for her feelings, just a sullen promise to resume his responsibilities, she thought. She would give a year of her life just to see his face when she told him where he could stuff his responsibilities. Her eyes clouded with fury, but she managed to bite back the words. The undoubted satisfaction she would receive wouldn't compensate for losing her dignity.

Instead, she kept her pride and moderated her voice as she replied, "That's just it, Hugh, you have nothing I want. I'll agree to giving you reasonable visitation rights with Jonathan, but you can put anything else out of your mind here and now."

"You always were a cold bitch," he snarled, his expression savage. "The only reason I could stomach the thought of having you back was because of Jonathan."

Her smile was mocking. "I'm glad you finally realize you don't have to go to such extremes."

"I'm warning you, Casey. Keep Walker away from my son!"

She watched Hugh storm through the fenced enclosure surrounding the pool, immensely relieved when he didn't stop to speak to Jonathan.

Hugh was right, she thought tiredly. He did hold an immense advantage, one he was evidently quite conscious of. The war he was waging wasn't over whether or not they remarried, she could see that now. His jealousy of Chad superseded all other considerations, and he would stop at nothing to score over a man he both envied and despised. She had rejected Hugh, but if he could see her now, her ex-husband would be tasting the sweetness of revenge. She had rid herself of one problem, only to be confronted with another. If Hugh acted on his jealousy, Jonathan was going to be as torn as a bone between two snarling dogs. The thought of the disillusionment and emotional scarring that could result didn't bear thinking of.

When Chad finally returned home, Casey had no opportunity to tell him about Hugh's jealousy of his relationship with Jonathan. It was immediately clear that Chad was seriously ill.

She had been working when Sally phoned, her voice ragged as she told Casey of Chad's condition.

"He stopped by the house to let us know he was back, and then he collapsed. "Oh, Casey!" Sally began to cry, loud, choking sobs that sent a shaft of fear through Casey's heart. "He's delirious, and he keeps calling for you."

The phone dropped from Casey's nerveless fingers and fell to the floor unnoticed. Luckily Marilyn was close by, and came to Casey's assistance when she swayed and would have fallen. It was then that Casey realized how much she loved him. Marilyn picked up the phone and, after listening to Sally for a moment, she replaced the receiver and turned to Casey. "You're in no condition to drive. Here's your purse. Sit here while I tell Sharon what's happened."

"I've got to go to him," Casey mumbled, having difficulty forming the words through stiff lips.

"Of course you do," Marilyn soothed, already turning away. "But I'll go with you."

During the days that followed, Casey was grateful for the support of her friends. The doctors had diagnosed pneumonia, and Casey became a familiar figure to the nurses at the hospital. She paced the corridors during the times she was banned from Chad's room, and spent the remaining hours seated at his bedside. She left only to sleep. Sally was caring for Jonathan, and she insisted that Casey use her guest room. She complied meekly, the thought of being alone in her own house abhorrent to her.

Jonathan was given an abbreviated description of Chad's illness, but they kept the seriousness of his condition from the child. Every day Casey promised to deliver the pictures Jonathan had drawn for Chad, and every day she prayed that the man she loved would open his eyes to see them. On the third day her prayers were answered, and when she saw the recognition in his drugged gaze, tears of joy and relief fell to dampen the hand she held tightly.

There was even laughter when he scowled at her bedraggled appearance and asked what the hell she'd been doing to herself. His voice was weak, but the aggressive slant to his mouth was the most welcome sight she'd ever encountered. Smiling, she lifted his hand to her cheek. "Shouldn't *I* be asking *you* that?"

"I've got a stupid cold," he muttered, brushing her mouth with his thumb. "Nothing to worry about."

"You neglected that stupid cold and ended up with pneumonia," she retorted, pressing a kiss against the fingers that moved to join his thumb in its caressing survey of her lips. "Why else do you think you're in the hospital, and not home where I can take care of you?"

"I want to go home with you, Casey."

She nodded, and cleared her throat before whispering gently, "I know you do."

His eyes closed wearily, and she saw his lips move as he began to drift into a healing sleep. She leaned forward, and agony twisted her insides as she heard him ask, "Do you also know how much I love you?"

8

Here we are, Mommy!"

Casey responded to her son's excited squeal with a wave of her hand. There was a smile on her lips as she watched the merry-go-round revolve. Jonathan and Chad were perched side by side on their noble steeds, pleasure evident in their flashing smiles. The three of them had spent most of the last two days relaxing on the beach, leaving their visit to the boardwalk until last. Keeping Chad and Jonathan away from the amusement park area of Santa Cruz hadn't been easy, she thought with a smile. Left to his own devices, Chad would have exhausted himself instead of taking things easy and regaining his strength after his long illness.

Her lips twitched in a wry grimace as she recalled the days following Chad's release from the hospital.

It had taken all of her persuasive powers and Sally's bullying to keep Chad confined to his bed. As his strength returned he had acted like a bear with a sore paw.

"I'm going nuts looking at these walls all day," he had complained, pacing the tile floors of his kitchen with discontent marring his handsome features.

Refusing to show a proper amount of sympathy for his plight, and piqued at being distracted every two minutes while she was trying to prepare a meal for them both, she snapped, "You know the doctor warned you about overdoing things."

"To hell with the doctor!"

"Honestly," she exclaimed, lifting a platter of sliced roast beef and carrying it to the table. "You're worse than a child."

He grinned at her frazzled expression and patted the top of her head. "Crying uncle, are you?"

"Oh, sit down and eat," she retorted, pulling out her chair and glaring at him as she followed her own advice.

"You know what we both need, Casey?"

"What?" she asked, ladling potatoes and carrots onto her plate.

"We need to get away for a while. Why don't we take Jonathan to Santa Cruz for a few days? It's a comfortable drive, and the weather's perfect for the beach."

"It sounds like heaven."

Her hands briefly tightened on the serving spoon as she considered her reply. To be alone with Chad and Jonathan away from the tensions and distractions of everyday living would be bliss. For a time she could put away the nagging worry over Jonathan's future that had been in the back of her mind since her confrontation with Hugh. Like Cinderella on her way to the ball, she was eager to escape into fantasy, however short her time of dreaming might be. Although she knew midnight would inevitably come, she would have had her hours with the prince.

"After dividing your time among Jon, the restaurant, and taking care of me, you're worn out."

His hand covered hers as she replaced the ladle at the side of the bowl, and Chad drew her fingers to his lips in a gesture of gratitude. "Let me take you away from it all for a while, little witch."

She heard the plea in his voice, and ached with the desire to give in to him. But she couldn't help remembering the menace in Hugh's eyes when he'd demanded that she keep Chad away from Jonathan, and she quailed at the prospect of adding fuel to the fire of his resentment. Since their conversation by the pool, Hugh hadn't returned to issue any further warnings, but she wasn't foolish enough to imagine he had given up. If anything, his absence increased her tension. He was playing a waiting game, using delaying tactics until he saw which way she was going to jump.

His repudiation of her had been the first honest emotion Hugh had shown since his return, she thought, feeling a surge of frustration as she realized the full extent of his self-centeredness. Everything Hugh had done in his life had been done on impulse, with little logic and even less emotion; she saw that now. They had married because Hugh had decided he needed a woman to provide his creature comforts; they had divorced because Susan could further his career; he had returned to California because he was on a losing streak and needed to use the family he'd discarded to bolster the pride Susan had hurt.

What a shock Chad must have been to him, she thought. Hugh had never once considered the possibility that anyone else might enter her life. He had gone away with Susan expecting Casey's world to stop turning in his absence. Hugh had discarded his toy with the thoughtlessness of a spoiled child, never expecting that someone else might pick it up. When confronted by a man like Chad, who had the prestige and financial success he had always craved for himself, Hugh's jealousy and spite were formidable. He didn't want her or Jonathan, but he was going to make certain Chad didn't get them either!

"There will be no strings attached, if that's what you're brooding about!" a harsh voice exclaimed.

She jumped, and lifted her head to encounter the hurt in Chad's eyes. Clearly, he had misconstrued the reason for her long silence. Her heartbeat faltered, and then continued more strongly than before. If he only knew, she thought, how much she was beginning to want those strings. But her desire didn't bear thinking about. She had refused his offer of marriage; she couldn't very well say that she would be willing to have an affair with him. She had to stand by her convictions. There was no other alternative, not if she wanted to keep her self-respect.

"Hey, Jon," Chad chuckled, jumping down from the merry-go-round. "I think Mommy's gone to cloud-cuckoo land."

Casey returned to the present with a jolt, momentarily disoriented as she watched Chad help Jonathan jump down from the now motionless merry-go-round. The two of them headed in her direction. "At least I didn't get there on a painted horse," she retorted. "I know better than to go around in a circle without getting anywhere."

"Then let's try the bumper cars," Chad suggested, his eyes dancing. "Jon and I will give you a run for your money."

"I haven't forgotten the way you two ganged up on me this morning," she retorted. "You bumped me into a corner and wouldn't let me out."

"Were we that mean to Mommy, Jon?"

Jonathan was an honest child; he enthusiastically nodded an affirmative. Casey sent a look of triumph in Chad's direction. "I rest my case," she laughed.

Chad glanced down at his thonged beach sandals, and grimaced. "Speaking of rest, what do you say to giving my feet a break?"

Casey made a face for Jonathan's benefit, and smiled when he giggled. "Your poor abused feet will have all the relaxation they need during the drive home. The way you two strong men look, the sooner you're tucked into bed the better."

"At least I won't wake up with bruises tomorrow morning," Chad retorted, taking a playful swipe at Jonathan's head. "Why didn't you tell me this little monster kicks in his sleep?"

"I offered to share with him," she remarked with studied innocence. "Anyway, you were the one who agreed to two rooms with one double bed apiece. If you hadn't insisted on adjoining accommodations, we wouldn't be having this discussion."

Chad bent closer, his whispered words for her ears alone. "Since you wouldn't share with me, I wanted you as close as possible. It was very comforting, listening to you snore through the door."

She slanted him a provocative glance from beneath her lashes. "You were obviously better off with Jonathan. My snoring would have kept you awake."

"That's a matter of opinion," he muttered, his mouth curving sensually as his eyes dropped toward the rounded neck of her blouse. "If I'd been sharing your bed, sleep would have been the last thing on my mind."

"I'm hungry!" Jonathan exclaimed.

Chad heard the petulance caused by tiredness in the little boy's voice, and pulled his fascinated gaze from the shimmering awareness in Casey's eyes. "So am I, son."

The double meaning wasn't lost on Casey, and

she flushed to the roots of her hair. Laughing with restored humor, Chad ruffled Jonathan's wind-tossed curls. "How does a hot dog sound, sport?"

"He should have a proper meal," Casey protested, hoping Chad would attribute the faint trembling in her voice to her efforts to keep up with his long-legged stride.

"Aw, Mom!"

At Jonathan's disgusted response, the two adults grinned at each other. "Don't argue with your mother, Jon."

Chad's gentle admonishment was ignored by the child. "But I want a hot dog, Chad."

"You want to grow up to be beautiful like Mommy, don't you?"

Jonathan snorted a protest. "No, I want to be big like you."

Chad responded to the telling statement by swooping down and lifting Jonathan onto his shoulders. There was pleasure in the eyes that sought Casey's. "Then you'll have a bowl of vegetable soup for Mommy, and a hot dog for me. Is that a good enough compromise, Casey?"

She wrinkled her nose, but softened her reaction with a smile. "That's a good enough compromise, Chad."

"Can I take Jon upstairs and put him to bed, Casey?"

Casey nodded, her expression tender as she took in the sight of her sleeping son curled up on Chad's lap. They had returned from Santa Cruz an hour before, after having stretched out their last day alone together as long as possible. Reluctant to part from him, Casey had invited Chad to stay for a last cup of coffee. An element of suppressed intimacy added a vibrant warmth to their conversation, and every time their eyes met Casey seemed to lose her breath.

There was a tautness to Chad's face whenever he looked at her that had her imagining herself poised on the brink of a chasm, where one move might send her hurtling to the bottom. In her usual fashion, Casey used activity to cover her reactions, but she never lost consciousness of the eyes that followed her as she busied herself with preparing their coffee. She was relieved when Jonathan began complaining about the sand trapped in his shoes, glad for the excuse to escape Chad's intense scrutiny.

After bathing the little boy and putting him into pajamas, Casey allowed Jonathan to return downstairs. Now, as she glanced down at his nearly full cup of hot chocolate, she wondered why she'd bothered. The bright blue plastic cup splattered with fading nursery-rhyme characters formed an odd contrast to the heavy brown mug sitting beside it, and her lips twisted humorously. Full of sea air and hot dogs, Jonathan hadn't taken two sips before succumbing to the sandman. Even his formidable, four-year-old willpower hadn't been strong enough to keep his eyes open.

With an ache in her breast Casey observed the expression on Chad's face as he rose slowly to his feet, careful not to disturb the sleeping child. He disappeared upstairs with Jonathan, and with a sigh she dropped her head against the back of the couch. She found herself giving in to the depression that had been threatening her happiness during the last few days. The ball is over, and Cinderella has lost much more than a slipper, she thought tiredly.

She was lethargically contemplating the bronze leaves of the metal sculpture hanging on the living room wall when a sound made her turn her head. The front door burst open, and her eyes widened in shock as she saw Hugh framed in the entrance. She jumped to her feet with an indignant exclamation. "Who do you think you are, walking in here unannounced?"

"Maybe it's time I showed you who I am!"

Casey tensed at the grim rejoinder, for the first time noticing the menace in Hugh's eyes. His cheeks were mottled with an angry flush, his expression bordering on violence. "Get out of here," she whispered, taking a tentative step backward.

He leaned back against the closed door with an ugly sneer. "You might as well get used to me," he remarked, icy control in his voice. "I'm not leaving here without my son."

She paled, her hand clutching at her throat. "Jonathan?"

At her exclamation, his eyes narrowed. "I'm not having him influenced by an immoral bitch like you."

"You're crazy," she whispered.

He thrust himself forward, his hands tensed as though he longed to hit her. "I warned you to keep Jonathan away from Walker, and you defied me by having a cozy weekend together. Well, I'm not going to stand for it, Casey."

"You just can't tolerate the idea of my having a life of my own, can you, Hugh? You don't want Jonathan," she muttered, "you never did."

"So maybe I've changed my mind regarding the joys of fatherhood," he said, a nasty twist to his lips. "Or maybe it's the thought of Walker taking over for me that sticks in my craw. Is he better in bed than I was, Casey?"

"Jonathan and I spent a few days with a friend," she retorted. "And might I remind you that I'm the one who has custody of our son?"

"That can be remedied by the courts, and probably will be when they learn what's going on. I suspected something like this when I called you from Chicago and that jerk answered the phone. But I thought you'd use a little discretion, and not be stupid enough to embroil my son in your sordid little games, Casey. He's growing up, and it won't take him long to figure out what's going on."

"And just what *is* going on, Delaney?"

Chad's voice reverberated from the stairwell, and Hugh stared in disbelief as the other man descended the steps. That Hugh was surprised by Chad's appearance was evidenced by the pallor that suddenly replaced the angry color in his face. "You know damn well what I'm talking about, you bastard!"

Chad moved to stand beside Casey, but she wasn't fooled by his deceptive calm. She was close enough to him to know that every muscle in his body had tightened, and she knew he was eager to release the violence in his coiled frame. "Chad, let me handle this," she murmured, placing a restraining hand on his arm.

He ignored her, his eyes on Hugh. "Why don't you spell it out," he encouraged softly, his eyes dangerous as he studied the other man. "I'm just itching to shove your teeth down your throat."

Casey closed her eyes and fought for control. Her stomach began to churn with nervousness, especially when Chad's hand covered her fingers to prevent her from moving away from him. Summoning what little patience she had remaining, she met Hugh's eyes.

"I think you've said enough," she remarked quietly. "I can't stop you from petitioning for custody of Jonathan, and I'm not afraid to have you try."

Hugh stood open-mouthed with incredulity, stunned by Casey's defiance. "You mean you'd risk losing your son because of a stupid affair?" he screeched, his expression conveying derision.

"It would take a little more than your vivid imagination to prove me unfit to care for my child," she retorted. "I'm well known in this town and can provide any number of character witnesses. I don't think you can say the same."

"Nevertheless," he spluttered indignantly, "I have a right to question the boy's upbringing."

"Your rights are all you're concerned with," she said, her eyes scathing as they searched his features. "You couldn't care less about Jonathan's feelings, as long as I don't dispute your authority."

"You don't know what you're talking about, Casey. Would I have offered to marry you, and give you and Jonathan my love and security if I . . . ?"

Chad had remained silent during this interchange, but at Hugh's pompous declaration he laughed mockingly. "You might be able to give them security," he snapped, "but you'll never have it in you to give them the love they need. If you did, you wouldn't have left them in the first place."

"Damn it, Chad!"

As she spoke, Casey turned to the man at her side, her anger channeled in his direction. "I'm the best judge of that!"

"That's right. Just stay out of this," Hugh demanded, his eyes flashing with triumph. "This is between Casey and me."

"You're wrong, you know."

Chad's gaze focused on Casey. "Isn't he, Katherine?"

Chad was playing the role of jealous lover to perfection, she thought bitterly. But she wasn't going to let herself be emotionally blackmailed by either man, and that was exactly what this situation amounted to. Hugh was using his position as Jonathan's father to influence her life, and in his own way Chad was just as guilty of trying to manipulate her. The expression on his face as he waited for her to affirm his claim clearly indicated his confidence that she belonged with him. Well, she had a mind of her own, she thought, gritting her teeth to stop herself from screaming. She didn't need some macho figure to make her decisions for her, and the sooner they both realized that, the better.

"Are you asking me a question, or making a statement, Chad?"

"You know how I feel about you, Casey."

"Oh, yes! I know how you feel, how Hugh feels, but have either of you bothered to consider my feelings?"

Hugh had the look of a man who'd reached down to pat a friendly dog only to be bitten. The tide had turned against him, and he was staring at Casey as though he'd never seen her before. Casey studied his bewildered features; it was like facing a stranger. For the first time she found herself close to hating him for the futility of the wasted years they'd spent together, years when he had suppressed her personality with his own.

Hugh tentatively reached out, but his hand fell at his side when she disdained his gesture, hunching her shoulders in unspoken rejection. He flushed with embarrassment, and sent a furtive glance in Chad's direction. "I'm damned if I'll just walk out of here and leave you to him."

"You don't have a choice," Chad snarled, clenching his fists at his sides. "I love Casey, and I intend to marry her. Go ahead with your threat, Delaney. As my wife, Casey will have all the protection she needs when she enters the court-room."

Casey didn't know who gasped the loudest, herself or Hugh. She turned incredulous eyes on Chad, and her heart contracted with anguish. She was being taken over by a will stronger than her own, and she didn't know what to do about it. Oh, God! Why had Chad placed her in this humiliating position? Didn't he understand the ramifications of his actions, or didn't he care as long as he got his own way? During the months they'd known each other she had come to believe that Chad respected her independence, when in reality he thought her as much in need of a strong man to cling to as her ex-husband.

Without respect, love was just an empty word. She didn't utter a sound as she walked to the door. When the knob turned beneath her hand, she turned to Hugh, her face drained of all emotion. "It's time you left."

"If you think I'm going to continue sending child support while you live it up with Walker, you're dreaming."

Chad stepped forward, his body under rigid control. "Unless you're willing to let me adopt him, you haven't much choice, Delaney," he responded, the disgust in his eyes belying the quietness of his voice.

"I don't give a damn what you and that bitch do," Hugh cried, lunging toward the door. "Just as long as you don't expect me to pay for it!"

Casey watched Hugh disappear down the path.

He was out of her life in a way she hadn't expected. She thought of the effect this was going to have on Jonathan, and as she turned toward Chad she felt guilty for the relief she felt. Taking a deep breath she prepared herself for what she had to do. "Please leave, Chad. I have no intention of marrying you, and under the circumstances I think it'll be better if we don't see each other anymore."

"You don't mean that, Casey!"

Some of her determination withered at the unbearable anguish in his voice, but she stood her ground. "I mean every word. I'm sorry it has to end this way."

"I love you, and I want to marry you," he exclaimed, bewilderment overlying the pain in his eyes. "Doesn't that mean anything to you?"

Tears filled her eyes, and she blinked rapidly to prevent their fall. "God help me," she whispered, "I love you, too."

The glow that suffused his face pierced her like a knife through her breast. But before he could close the distance separating them, she lifted her hand in a defensive gesture and motioned him away. "It's no good, Chad."

He frowned, but halted his approach. "I don't understand."

"I know you don't." The whispered admission released her tears, and angrily she brushed the moisture from her cheeks.

"Then tell me," he demanded, moving forward swiftly and reaching out for her. When she made no attempt to move away he rested his chin against the top of her head, and wrapped his arms around her trembling body. "I love you so much, honey. I want to take care of you and Jonathan; to give you all the things in life you both deserve."

She laughed, and felt him stiffen at the bitterness of the sound. "You want to care for me as long as my wants coincide with what you yourself think and feel. You've proven that tonight. But that isn't enough for me, and it never will be. The one thing Hugh did for me when he left was to make me face up to my own weaknesses. I know now that I can't marry you."

Casey took a backward step so that she could look into his eyes and gauge his reaction. "When I married Hugh I ignored my real feelings, convincing myself I loved him because I wanted to be in love. I tried to be what he wanted me to be, until I couldn't think or act for myself. For more years than I care to remember I resented him, and I hated myself. Well, I'm not prepared to live like that again. A new person has emerged from the ashes of that dead relationship. She's someone I'm just beginning to know, and although I don't always like the discoveries I make, I'm free to assimilate the changes I feel in myself. I won't risk that freedom by loving you. I didn't ask you to walk into my life, and I know you have too much pride to stay where you're not wanted.

"Don't you understand," she finally cried, pressing her fingers against her eyes to shut out the sight of his pain. She swallowed and drew in her breath sharply. "I'm sorry if you're disappointed by what

I'm telling you, but it's better to be disillusioned now than later."

A muscle throbbed in Chad's jaw. "No one with the courage to love has any guarantees, Katherine."

Casey summoned all her strength of will to speak the next words. "But you see, I'm really very much a coward, Chad."

9

Casey marked the last ounce of cheese off the itemized list of supplies she held in her hand, and needlessly rechecked the van's refrigeration system. She moved about the compact quarters of their mobile catering unit restlessly, trying to concentrate her attention on the job at hand. She usually considered stocking fresh supplies before a party more of a pleasure than a chore, yet lately even the simplest of familiar tasks seemed to increase her dissatisfaction with life in general.

Retracing her steps to the rear of the restaurant, she wondered if she would ever regain her enthusiasm for her career. Not just her career, she admitted realistically. Somehow every aspect of her life seemed barren, with Jonathan the only bright spot on her horizon.

Poor little Jonathan, she thought, clenching her teeth tightly when she thought of Hugh's thoughtless cruelty toward their son. A light mist began to fall from the storm clouds threatening overhead, and she tilted her head back to allow the drizzle to cool her heated cheeks. She breathed deeply of the salt-laden air.

Hugh didn't really think of himself as a cruel man, she realized. With a childish selfishness even Jonathan was beginning to outgrow, Hugh related to others only in terms of what was best for himself. That was why he had again disappeared from their lives with a callous suddenness that left the little boy wondering why his daddy hadn't liked him enough to stay. In trying to make Jonathan understand, she, too, had finally opened her mind to the truth. It had taken her a long time to see Hugh for the weak, ineffectual man he really was, she thought, and not as some monster conjured up by her imagination. She supposed it was a step in the right direction.

Her feet lagged as she lifted exhausted eyes toward a sky as gloomy as her thoughts. Nature was using the darkest colors of her palette to paint the inevitability of winter's approach, and the thought saddened her. She didn't like living in summer's shadow. She desperately wanted to go backward in time to experience again bright blue skies and warm nights when the moon hung in the sky like a child's runaway balloon. It had been a summer's eve when Chad entered her life, she remembered. She bit her lip, and tears stung her blinking eyelids. And it had been a summer's eve when she had finally sent him away.

"Sharon, I'm leaving now," she called, as she pushed aside the heavy door opening into the kitchen. "The van's loaded, and I'll pick the others up on my way to Piedmont."

"What's your hurry?" Sharon replied shortly. "You've time to share a cup of coffee with me before you leave."

Casey knew her friend well enough to suspect that coffee wasn't the only thing on her mind. The other woman hadn't tried to hide her disapproval of the hours Casey had been putting in at the restaurant, and she knew from the look on Sharon's face that she wasn't going to avoid an explanation of her behavior for much longer. Both Sharon and Marilyn had voiced their worry on numerous occasions, and although she appreciated their concern, Casey had known she would find no relief in sharing her troubles with her friends. The misery eating away inside her went too deep for words, and nothing anyone could say was going to miraculously turn her life around.

Trying her best to summon a smile, she followed Sharon from the kitchen and seated herself at a small round table with a tired sigh. She glanced around the restaurant, finding the echoing emptiness oppressive. She needed people and noise and laughter to dispel the loneliness of the world she had created for herself. There was a potted fern beside the table, and as Sharon went to get their coffee, Casey studied the leaves with more concentration than the plant warranted. The nursery that stocked these rooms with greenery was due to pick up this ailing specimen on Monday. She traced a mottled brown stain with her finger, and wondered if the plant was dying from lack of attention. Did people, too, die slowly inside, when there was no longer a loving hand to soothe away the pain, or a gentle voice to offer affection?

"Go ahead and cry, Casey," a soft voice whispered at her side. "I think it's time you learned to release your emotions instead of locking them away inside you."

Casey shook her head violently and reached for the cup of coffee Sharon set on the table in front of her. "Tears won't solve anything."

"Not by themselves . . . no."

There was a tremor in Sharon's voice, and Casey looked up at her in surprise. Her friend pulled out a chair and lowered her body into its cushioned softness with an air of weariness. "Only when we try to understand our grief and deal with it do tears cleanse our souls, Casey."

"You don't understand," Casey responded impatiently.

"But I do," Sharon sighed, her gaze drawn inward. "I know that you and Marilyn think I've remained single because of a misguided sense of duty to my family, but you're wrong. It's true that when I was eighteen I joined the army to help support my brothers and sisters, and I've thanked

156

God on my knees for my sacrifice. If I had remained at home I would never have met the man I still love more than life itself. That's why I get so impatient with Marilyn when she tries to matchmake. A long time ago I made my own choice, and I know that for me there will never be anyone to take Michael's place in my heart."

A knot of emotion formed in Casey's throat at the certainty in Sharon's words. "What happened?" she whispered.

"His company was one of the last to be sent to Vietnam."

Casey didn't have to ask the question hovering in her mind. She saw the answer in Sharon's eyes. "I'm so sorry."

Sharon smiled and shook her head in gentle admonishment. "Don't be sorry for me," she said, her low voice holding underlying meaning as she rose to her feet. "The night before Michael left we went to a hotel together. We spoke of our love with our bodies, and with our lips we spun dreams of a future together. The arms that held me blocked out the fear of what tomorrow might bring and gave me the strength to go on without him."

"Why have you told me about Michael when even your own sister doesn't know?"

"Because you are the one who is afraid, not Marilyn. You have yet to learn that with strong arms around you it's possible to face life with courage. Even when those arms are removed and the dreams are gone, nothing can take away the memories. There's still a chance for you, as long as you remember that love enriches; it doesn't destroy. Only people can do that to themselves, Casey."

A tight ache of emotion lodged in Casey's chest as she watched Sharon walk away. There was serenity in her bearing and unconscious pride in her retreating figure. Sharon wasn't burdened by a fear of the future. Although she had lost Michael, she still held dear the love he had given her. In a way, of the two of them, Sharon was the one to be envied, she thought, her body moving mechanically toward the rear exit of the restaurant. Sharon had known how to give her love freely. Unlike Casey, she didn't have anything to reproach herself for.

Casey was fitting the key into the door of the van when memory overtook her: *I'm really very much a coward, Chad.*

Dear God, when would those words cease to haunt her? Were they locked forever in her subconscious, a constant reminder of her own cowardice? She remembered a long-ago incident. She had been roller-skating in front of her home and had tripped over a crack in the sidewalk. She'd lain sobbing, her knee skinned and her pride in tatters, when her brother arrived to give her some much-needed sympathy.

"It hurts, Bobby," she had cried. "It hurts real bad!"

He grinned and gave her a hug. "Want a magic kiss, Casey?"

She wiped the tears from her eyes and waited until he placed his mouth gently against the abrasion. As he carried her into the house to have it cleaned, the worst of the pain had been forgotten. If only her family wasn't hundreds of miles away. Oh, Bobby! I need you now, she cried silently, as she climbed into the bucket seat of the van and tightened the safety belt around her waist. It hurts real bad, and there's no one here to kiss away the pain.

Chad adjusted the catcher's mitt to fit Jonathan's hand and winked his encouragement before he stepped back a short distance and bounced the baseball in his palm. A familiar ache began in the region of his chest as he noted the look of determination on the youngster's face. In that instant Jonathan's likeness to his mother was so obvious that Chad felt ravaged by the despair he'd lived with for so long.

There had been days when he hadn't caught even a glimpse of Casey, and they had been marked off in his mind as empty and meaningless. But they hadn't been the worst moments; those had come when he encountered her unexpectedly. Then he had been compelled by the wariness in her eyes to greet her like a casual acquaintance. Every time this happened he felt as though he betrayed the love he had for her, and it hurt. But she gave him no other alternative, he thought.

The frustration that was never far from the surface twisted his features. God, how he hated the defensive way she responded to his tentative greetings. It made him feel helpless to bridge the wall she'd erected between them.

"Throw the ball now, Chad," Jonathan pleaded, his small feet in scuffed Nikes shifting restlessly on the well-manicured lawn.

"Think you're ready for my fast ball, hotshot?"

A nervous giggle was Jonathan's only response. A brisk wind flirted with the boy's hair, lifting and ruffling his dark curls. His lightweight, blue nylon Windbreaker was plastered against his slight frame as another gust dipped over the surrounding hills. Chad noted the smell of moisture permeating the air with a feeling of depression. It was the scent of fall, and as he observed the billowing gray clouds scudding across the sky, he realized that summer was nearly over.

Where had they gone, those hot, brilliant blue days he had welcomed with such eagerness, he wondered. He no longer woke each morning with the hope of being with Casey. His only pleasure was the time he spent with Jon, and the honest affection he received from the child soothed the hurt that had been inflicted by the boy's mother.

Every night when he got home after work, Jonathan would run from Sally's to greet him, and the burden of loneliness Chad carried would be eased by his company. Soon, though, even that small consolation would be denied him, he realized. The days were shortening as winter approached, and eventually he would be coming home without the sun to light his way. Jon wouldn't be allowed outside after dark, and he knew his isolation would then be complete.

Damn it, Walker! He mentally cursed his depression. When are you going to stop feeling sorry for yourself and get on with your life? Hell, man . . . there are other women in the world. Women who could ease your frustration, an insidious inner voice whispered. Women with rounded, smooth-skinned bodies, and eyes that promise the forgetfulness to be found in their arms. He tried to concentrate his attention on visualizing a featureless head on his pillow; soft arms lifting to pull him down until his aching flesh merged with comforting warmth. When the image focused in his mind, he shook his head to dispel the illusion. It was Casey's face he saw.

"Aren't we going to play catch anymore, Chad?"

Chad shook his head, his jaw clenching briefly as he looked at Jonathan. "I think we'd better call it a day, son."

Son! God, he felt like his insides were being wrenched apart when he noticed the boy's downcast expression. Jonathan's face had crumpled into the same guarded look Chad had so often seen on Casey's. He resisted the impulse to demand a reason for the boy's abrupt change of mood. He wasn't a mind reader, for God's sake! He was tired of trying to second-guess the mother, and he was damned if he was going to start with the son.

"Come on, let's head for my place and I'll fix us some hot chocolate."

Inwardly wincing at the impatience in his voice, he shortened his stride so Jonathan could keep up. As he glanced over his shoulder, he saw the hesitancy on the boy's face, and hated himself for allowing his bad humor to affect an innocent child. None of this was Jon's fault, he thought. Chad's jaw ached with tension, but he managed to issue a challenge that he knew would elicit an immediate response.

"Race you to the door, sport!"

Fifteen minutes later Chad carried two mugs of hot chocolate from the kitchen to the front room. As he passed the television, he turned it on and automatically switched the channel to a station airing cartoons. His preference ran to the six o'clock news, but he usually settled for Bugs Bunny. Since Casey seemed to be putting almost all of her evenings into her duties at the restaurant, he usually returned Jon to Sally's for dinner at six-thirty. It was a convenient pattern, he decided bitterly. Casey had most mornings and afternoons free to spend with her son, Sally had the evenings, and thanks to the understanding heart of that kind lady, he had one single, stolen hour.

He seated himself on the rug beside Jon with a groan, and they sat with their backs braced against the bottom of the couch. He lifted his mug to his mouth and grimaced as the heat seared his tongue. He noticed that Jonathan's mug, cooled with an extra helping of milk, sat untasted on the coffee table in front of them.

"Better drink up, sport," he said with forced jocularity. "It'll be time to head for Sally's soon."

"Can't I spend the night, Chad?"

Chad tried not to show how much the idea appealed to him. Tomorrow was Saturday, and he could take Jon to the park while Casey caught up on her sleep. She would be awake by the time he brought her son home, and she would probably be prompted by politeness to offer him a cup of coffee. She might even agree to the three of them going out to lunch together, and . . . He caught hold of his thoughts, disgust at his own duplicity flooding through him.

His love for the son wasn't dependent on the feverish obsession he felt for the mother, and he was damned if he would let himself use Jonathan as a wedge. It was bad enough that the boy's father had used that ploy. The callous bastard, he thought viciously. According to Sally, Hugh had gotten his revenge on Casey through Jonathan. Jon was a sensitive little soul, and bright for his age. It hadn't taken him long to stop asking why his daddy didn't come to see him anymore.

Chad turned his eyes to the boy at his side. As he absorbed the trusting eagerness in the small face, he cleared his throat to ease the ache of emotion lodged there. "Not without your mother's permission, Jon."

Chad expected a show of disappointment, and was startled when Jon blurted, "I could stay if Mommy said it was all right?"

"Of course," he replied absently. He knew Casey was aware of the time Jonathan spent with him, but he didn't know how she felt about the closeness developing between himself and her son. But then his features softened with tenderness. She loved Jon too much to deny him the male companionship he craved, no matter how she was affected by the relationship. There was no selfishness in Casey, he thought with pride, even though she guarded her own emotional privacy so zealousy.

"Can we have popcorn and stay up real late?"

Jonathan had jumped to his feet and was whirling around the room like a small tornado. "Hey, hold on a minute," Chad cautioned.

"I can stay . . . Mommy said I could spend the night if you asked me sometime."

Chad grinned, realizing he'd just been had. "I guess I could check with Sally."

Jonathan pulled him to his feet. When Chad made a teasing show of reluctance, Jon slipped behind him and pushed him toward the phone. Some of the boy's excited anticipation spilled over into him, and he was grinning as he dialed Sally's number. But the smile on his face faltered when he heard the reservation in the older woman's voice.

"I don't know, Chad. Casey never said anything to me about Jonathan spending the night at your place. I'm sure she wouldn't mind, but . . ."

"According to Jon, she's already given her permission," he said.

Jonathan was standing quietly beside him, and the tears of disappointment building in the boy's eyes spurred Chad's determination. "Look, I can understand your position, Sally. Why don't I call Casey at the restaurant, and get back to you?"

There was a moment of hesitation on the other end of the line before Sally's laughter broke the silence. "I'm being foolish. Casey's working a catering job tonight, and I wouldn't want to phone unless it was an emergency. Jonathan did say something to me yesterday about his mother letting him spend the night with you. But as usual Casey was in such a rush this afternoon I forgot to ask her. Anyway, if I know our Jonathan the question is academic at this point. I have a hunch that you didn't even know about this sleep-over until a few minutes ago. Am I right?"

"Sally, you're a mind reader."

"Not a bit of it," she said briskly. "I don't believe in all that supernatural claptrap, but I do know Jonathan. I'll pin a note to Casey's door and let her know you've agreed to keep him."

"Thanks, Sally," he said, chuckling when Jonathan responded to his affirmative nod with a yell. "As you can hear, I'm going to have my hands full."

"Well, why don't you two head over here for dinner?" she suggested. "I've made a stew, and there's plenty to go around."

"I appreciate the invitation, but Jon and I are going to play at being self-sufficient bachelors tonight. We might as well make hay while the sun shines."

"Humph," she snorted, her voice laden with unexpected emotion. "And it rises and sets in that boy and his mother, doesn't it, Chad Walker?"

Chad's hand tightened around the receiver. "I guess I'm a pretty transparent kind of a guy."

"Too much so for your own good!"

Her retort held impatience and undisguised disapproval. "I'm an interfering old busybody. But that's never stopped me from speaking my mind, and I'm not about to let it now. You and that stubborn girl were meant for each other."

"I know," he agreed heavily. "I tried to tell her, but she's not listening, Sal."

"Maybe you've used the wrong words, or maybe you shouldn't have used words at all. Honestly," she complained, "sometimes the younger generation fills me with dread. In my time we wouldn't have pussyfooted around, afraid to step on each other's toes."

Chad laughed and assumed a shocked tone. "What are you suggesting, you wicked woman?"

Sally's giggle was almost girlish. "You're man enough to know very well what I mean. I, unlike some people I could mention, am not in the habit of wasting my breath unless engaged in strenuous physical activity."

Chad choked and then gasped into the phone. "No wonder Bill looks at you all funny sometimes!"

"If you'd give Casey a few funny looks yourself," she snapped, "you might manage to get somewhere."

"I promise to give some serious thought to your wise if degenerate advice, my love."

"You save that for her, young man!"

"I will," he whispered, the words a promise he suddenly knew he had to keep if he hoped to cling to his sanity. His mouth curved with unconscious sensuality as he replaced the receiver in its cradle, then exuberantly bent down to lift Jonathan high in the air. Their combined laughter sounded triumphant.

Jonathan's late night never materialized. After his shower he emerged from Chad's bathroom yawning widely. By the time Chad dressed him in an old football jersey pulled from the back of his closet, and allowed him to splash on some of his aftershave, Jonathan was dazed but happy. Chad didn't think the meal he and Jonathan prepared together would have met with Casey's approval. But Jonathan acted as though two hot dogs, a can of Coke, and a bowl of popcorn were a feast fit for the gods. To his delight they indulged their appetites on the carpet in front of the television, something his mother never allowed. As Jonathan's sleepiness finally got the better of him, all was right in his world.

Nothing was right in Casey's world. Her crew had catered a bachelor party that evening, and had suffered the indignity of being treated as part of the entertainment. The beautifully prepared dishes were wasted on the men who hovered near the open bar, and the few who staggered in their direction were more interested in making insulting propositions than eating. Now, as she read the note Sally had taped to her door, her control broke.

She was exhausted, and soaking wet from the rain that had started during the evening. Returning home to discover that her son was spending the night with Chad was the last straw. As she spun on her heel and headed next door, she didn't stop to consider why her rage was directed solely at Chad. She had spent too many nights staring into the darkness, her whole body aching with longing for him.

"Casey, what are you . . . ?"

Chad's greeting faltered when Casey rudely pushed her way past him.

"Where's Jonathan?" she demanded, tapping her foot impatiently against the carpet as he closed the door.

"Asleep in the guest bedroom."

She was dripping rainwater and Chad stared at her with an expression of concern. "Is anything wrong?"

Despite her anger, she was aware of his masculine appeal. His hair glistened damply from a recent shower, and the robe he wore parted to reveal an intriguing tangle of hair covering his chest. Involuntarily her eyes glided down to where the luxurious mat narrowed and disappeared beneath the loosely knotted belt at his waist. When her glance encountered bare legs and feet, she flushed at the thought of the nakedness the robe covered. Embarrassment brought about a resurgence of her anger.

"Just how long has this been going on?"

He frowned, exasperation glinting in his eyes as he ran a hand through his already disordered hair. "If I knew what you were referring to, I might be able to answer your question."

"You know very well what I'm getting at, Chad."

"Look," he muttered impatiently. "If you're mad

because I let Jonathan spend the night at my place, then I'm sorry. He told me you'd OK'd the idea."

"You always believe everything a four-year-old tells you?"

His face darkened at her sarcastic jibe. "Jon doesn't lie!"

Disconcerted by his immediate defense of her son, she hesitated. "That's not the point."

"Then what is?" His temper was evident in the brevity of his question.

"When Jonathan mentioned spending the night with you, I avoided giving him a direct answer. He's been disappointed enough by his father, and I counted on you to show a little discretion."

"What the hell does discretion have to do with Jon spending the night? I'm perfectly capable of seeing he comes to no harm and I'm damned if I'm going to hurt his feelings by pandering to your desire to keep yourself separate from the rest of us ordinary mortals."

"Even under pressure from Hugh I never tried to discourage your friendship with Jon, but this is the last time you're going to usurp my authority with my own son. I provide excellent care for him while I'm at work and I don't appreciate returning home to find him with you."

"That sounded as if there was a threat in there somewhere." His eyes narrowed, and his voice held a lash of indignation as he questioned her. "Are you threatening me, Casey?"

"You're damn right I am," she said. "Jonathan

loves you too much already, and I've got to protect him, Chad. If he becomes any more attached to you than he already is, it's going to hurt him unbearably when you leave."

"Are you so certain I'll leave?"

"Of course you will," she scoffed, her body held rigid as she faced him. "After the novelty passes you'll get on with your own life, and Jonathan will be desolate."

"Only Jonathan . . . or will you be desolate, too?"

He moved closer, a disturbing message in his eyes. "That's been your trouble right along, Casey. You're so insecure you never learned to place any value on yourself. Then, when you finally found the courage to break out of your shell, you ended up alone, didn't you? That was the price you paid for your independence, wasn't it?"

"You're wrong," she muttered bitterly. "It was only when I was alone that I had the freedom to be myself."

"Like hell it was!"

Before she knew what was happening she was enclosed in unrelenting arms and pressed against a body that shook with emotion. "You place so much store in freedom," he said, his eyes flashing while the color came up under his skin, "and yet you've never really experienced it. You're still trapped by your own negative attitude, Casey."

She pressed her palms against his chest, then nearly fell when he suddenly released her with an exclamation of disgust. As he crossed the room to lean against the banister rail leading upstairs, she stared at him uncertainly. "You don't know what you're talking about, and I'm too tired to try to reason with you at the moment. I don't have to justify the way I choose to live my life, to you or anyone else."

"Is that your definition of freedom?"

She nodded defiantly, and winced when his harsh laughter grated on her overwrought nerves. "Have you ever heard of compromise?" he asked tiredly. "One of the dictionary definitions is to 'bind by agreement.' To bind together is one of life's positives, Katherine."

"Compromise also means to endanger," she whispered.

He shifted his weight restlessly, but his eyes remained locked with hers. "How do you define love, Casey? Isn't it a voluntary binding together of two individuals?"

"Yes, but . . ."

"Then to love is to compromise our emotions, and that means we can't escape the threat of danger. We're left vulnerable and exposed to the people we love, and maybe that's the way it should be.

"I'll take you upstairs now, Casey," he said, his tone one of defeat. "But when you look at your son examine your feelings for him. Because whether you know it or not, you've sacrificed some of your precious freedom for that boy. The loss has never been felt because it's been replaced with something of greater value—the only commodity in life that can't be bought, or borrowed, or stolen. It's time you realized you can't minimize the value of love by rejecting it, Casey. We're far richer when it's given away."

He motioned for her to precede him up the stairs, and she complied as though compelled by the tension in his body. She entered the room where Jonathan slept alone, but was ever conscious of the shadowy figure who hovered in the open doorway. She tried to blank out the words he had spoken, unable to bear the thought of how much she had already sacrificed.

Chad was right, she realized dully. All her life she had resented the restrictions placed upon her in the name of love. Instead of attempting to understand what motivated her father and brothers, she had opted for the easy way out. She had placed conditions on her love for them; later, she had restricted the feelings she had for Hugh. As she gazed into the sleeping face of her son, she finally understood the full extent of her own selfishness.

Love had to be given unconditionally if it was to reach its fullest potential. Slowly lifting her head, she searched the doorway for Chad. He was gone. Now she understood the message behind Sharon's story. She had been trying to show Casey the greatest freedom of all. It was called love—and she had tossed it ruthlessly aside without ever understanding its beauty.

10

With a muffled sob Casey fell to her knees beside Jonathan, and drew his sleep-warmed body into her arms. She buried her face against his neck and trembled when the aroma of the pine-scented after-shave Chad favored permeated her senses. A picture of her son carefully emulating Chad's shaving ritual rose in her mind, and she ached with guilt for wanting to deny him the guidance of a man he adored.

"G'night, Mommy."

She fussily rearranged his covers as she struggled to control her emotions. "Sweet dreams, darling.

"I'm glad you had a good time with Chad tonight," she continued in a whisper, brushing a soft kiss against his forehead.

He sighed with remembered pleasure, and rolled over onto his stomach. "I wish he was my daddy."

He didn't see the stricken expression on his mother's face. His lashes fluttered briefly and then rested like a silken fan against his cheeks. For long moments Casey watched him while he slept. His final words echoed in her brain, until her heart picked up the refrain and embellished it with a similar wish of her own.

She wasn't aware of her cramped limbs as she remained beside her son. Only the cleansing tears that trickled from her eyes held any reality. When tender arms lifted her to her feet, she didn't even try to protest their authority. She went with Chad willingly, at last able to lean on him for the emotional support she craved with every fiber of her being.

"I'm not leaving you alone tonight."

Her pulse pounded madly at his words, until he qualified his statement by muttering, "You can use my bed. I'll sleep downstairs on the couch."

She clamped her hands around his upper arms, and trembled violently with the need to speak. Entreating words formed in her mind as he walked with her down the hallway to the open door of his bedroom, and she cursed herself for her inability to say them aloud. She glanced over at the bed, the covers turned down invitingly, and her shaking increased until her teeth chattered in reaction.

"God, you're as cold as ice," Chad exclaimed, drawing her closer in an attempt to infuse her body with his warmth. "The rain's coming down in buckets outside, and you go to work in a damn flimsy sweater!"

At his accusing growl, she attempted to be conciliatory. "It wasn't raining when I left home."

"You'll be lucky if you don't end up with pneumonia." He grabbed her hand and led her into the bathroom opening off his bedroom. "I've got an extra robe hanging behind the door. Take those clothes off and get into the bath. I'll go downstairs and fix you a hot whiskey and lemon."

He was gone before she could respond to his peremptory demands, not that she would have protested. It felt so good to be fussed over by someone who cared whether or not she expired as a result of her drenching, she thought. She waited to experience resentment at having Chad dictate her actions, but felt only a glowing warmth.

While the tub filled she discarded her clothing in a damp heap on the floor and immediately stepped into the tub. The hot water rose around her as she lay back with closed eyes, and only when it reached her breasts did she rouse herself enough to turn the faucets off. She reached for the soap and began to lather her skin. She didn't dare lie down again, she thought, her mouth curving sensually. She remembered only too well what had happened the last time.

Wouldn't that be the easiest solution to the problem? she asked herself. Chad would eventually come to check on her as he had before, and his eyes and hands would be tempted by her nakedness. Even in his anger tonight she had seen desire, and she knew his control was rapidly evaporating. His emotions this evening had been heightened by their argument, and any further taunting on her part would send him over the edge of reasonable behavior.

Yes, he would take what she no longer wanted to withhold from him, she realized. But in so doing she would be denying him the one thing he needed most—a willing acknowledgment of the love she felt for him. If all he had wanted from her was her body, she finally allowed herself to admit, he would have achieved his purpose long ago. He was experienced enough to know that the physical attraction between them was far from one-sided.

It would have been so easy for him to use sex as the key to unlocking her emotions, she thought achingly. But he had been courageous enough to risk losing her by giving her time to discover the depth of her own feelings toward him. An inbred integrity hadn't allowed him to win by coercion what she wouldn't give him by choice. So he had remained in the background of her life . . . and waited. That was why she had fought against giving in to her feelings for him for so long. Because in her heart she'd known he needed more than a surface relationship, and she hadn't had the confidence to believe herself capable of giving him what he wanted.

Dear God! She was still terrified of failure, but at last she had a reason to try to overcome her fear. Chad had given her the courage she needed. She didn't know, any more than he did, what the future held for them. All she was sure of was her love for him and his for her.

Casey lowered her head. She inspected with detachment her exposed flesh. Her skin was smooth and supple; her legs, although not long, were well proportioned. Her small waist made her hips seem fuller and her breasts were firm and rounded, if not as voluptuously generous as she would have wished. Chad had seen her naked, if only briefly, and had praised her body. She longed to have him do so again . . . tonight.

Her thoughts in seething confusion, she automatically lathered her hair with the shampoo she found on the inner ledge of the bath. After draining the water from the tub, she closed the shower curtain and adjusted the shower head until a heavy spray rinsed the soapy residue from her hair and skin. She jumped when Chad's voice called from the other side of the door.

"If you need them, you'll find a brush and a blow dryer in the cabinet under the basin."

She croaked a thank you and hurriedly reached for the bath towel on an adjacent rail. His resonant tones made her shake with something other than coldness. Her nakedness caused a sensation of heat to sweep over her skin. Drying herself haphazardly, she hastily wrapped the heavy terry cloth around herself.

Catching a glimpse of her face in the mirror as she brushed and dried her hair, she was startled by the softness of her expression. But she wasn't dismayed by the glow of anticipation in her eyes. She looked like what she was, she thought dreamily. A woman not only willing, but also eager to be made love to by the man of her choice. The thought replaced her nervousness with determination, and she reached for the robe with a hand that only trembled slightly.

The bedroom suited Chad. She stood in the doorway and studied her surroundings. She'd been too distracted to notice the room when he'd led her into the bath. The walls were bone white as were her own, but there the similarity ended. Bold abstract prints embellished the stark surfaces with needed color, and the sheets and heavy comforter covering the bed picked up several of the shades in the pictures.

It was a "spool" bed; the turned wooden posts of polished oak were fashioned in a country style that was enormously pleasing to her eye. Slowly she moved forward and ran her hand appreciatively over a single carved post. She smiled as she considered the seemingly endless length of the mattress. It was certainly the right size for a man of Chad's proportions, and she giggled nervously at the thought of how ridiculous she would look surrounded by so much sumptuous comfort.

"Here's that drink I promised you."

Casey whirled in shock to face the doorway opening onto the hall, her mouth suddenly drying with apprehension. His body looked strong and imposing with only the tightly belted terry robe covering his nakedness. The eyes that studied her held a wary tension, and she frowned uneasily until the truth hit her with the force of a blow. Her silence was making him nervous! At this sign of his vulnerability, her eyes glistened with emotion.

"I don't want a drink, Chad," she murmured gently, reaching beside her to casually stroke the comforter covering the bed. As she absorbed the silky feel of the coverlet, her eyes remained on his face with hungry intensity. She saw his glance slide down her arm, his attention riveted on the sensual motion of her fingers.

His jaw flexed and his face became a brooding mask of frustration. "Then I'll leave you to sleep."

She heard the harsh indecisiveness in his voice and smiled. "Is that what you want? To leave me alone in this big bed?"

"For God's sake don't torment me," he gasped, lifting tortured eyes to her face.

With every evidence of anger he deposited the drink he still held on the modular bookshelf that hung on the wall at his side. But Casey was aware of the violent tremor that shook his fingers as they released the mug, just as she was aware of the reason for the terse expletive he uttered when some of the liquid slopped over the ceramic lip.

It was this awareness that overcame her self-consciousness, and empathy for the pain in his voice gave her the courage to finally break down the barriers that existed between them. He had his back to her, his hands braced on either side of the door frame, as if he was trying to summon the strength to walk away. When his slumped shoulders straightened with rigid control, every inch of her responded to the urgency of the moment.

"I don't want to sleep here without you, Chad," she whispered, the words a dry rasp in her throat. "Please, don't leave me. I . . . I don't want to be alone."

He whirled around, his mouth a slash against the paleness of his face. "You don't know what you're asking!"

The hoarse reproof momentarily sapped her confidence, until she realized the interpretation he'd placed on her request. He thought she was seeking a companion to chase away the disturbing darkness of the night, as though she were a child in need of comfort. Locking her eyes on his, she responded with total honesty.

"I'm asking you to make love to me."

His hand grasped the edge of the door, his knuckles whitened from the force of his grip. She saw his Adam's apple move as he swallowed, but his feverish gaze never left her face. "Do you really want my love, Casey?" He lessened the distance separating them with a single step. "Or just sex?" he concluded cruelly.

"Chad, don't!"

He stopped, his face anguished as he saw the wounded look in her eyes. "God, don't look at me with fear," he gasped, releasing the door to lift his hand in silent appeal. "I can take anything from you but that, Casey. For a minute I hoped . . ." His breathing was unsteady. "I'm such a gullible fool where you're concerned."

She started at his angry tone, her eyes revealing her confusion. "What do you mean?"

At her cry, the anger drained from his expression, and he observed her bewilderment with sadness. "I attacked you tonight, Casey. Not just now," he sighed, shaking his head, "but from the minute you walked through my door. I . . . you'll never know how much I regret my actions. But there's no need to defend your ability to love by sacrificing your body."

"You know I love you, Chad."

He shook his head, his mouth curved in a wry grimace. "You don't tell a man you love him and then shove him out the door, honey. There's no way he's going to believe you really want him given those circumstances."

"But I do," she gasped, lifting her hand in a gesture of appeal. "I do want you!"

"To prove to yourself you're desirable, not the failure in bed your husband made you out to be?" He closed his eyes and released his breath in a shuddering groan. "You don't need me for that, Katherine. Just search inside yourself for the sensuality you've kept suppressed for so long. You have to accept that what you thought of as failure was really a form of self-preservation from your husband. He's the one without the ability to love, don't you understand?"

His lashes lifted to reveal the passionate intensity of his gaze, while his mouth curved into a smile of encouragement. "No matter what I said tonight, I've always recognized your loving heart, little witch. That's what I saw in your eyes the first time I looked at you. But the loving was buried so deeply beneath a shadow of disillusionment that I couldn't reach you. Oh, God," he groaned. "How I wanted to set you free—free to love me as much as I love you!"

"And now you're the one who doesn't understand, Chad. I'm not frightened to love you any longer. Ever since I was a shy, insecure adolescent I've demanded my freedom at the expense of love. It was you who made me realize I'd trapped myself into a spiritual loneliness with my attitude.

"You've shown me so much," she admitted, her eyes imploring with the shining purity of brilliant green emeralds. "Now show me how to express the love I have for you with actions as well as words. You're right, I am afraid of disappointing you, the way I . . ."

Her words faltered, but then continued in a rush of released emotion. "But I love you too much to use you to settle any old scores, Chad. Please, can't you believe that, and just be patient with me a little longer?"

The door was pushed closed and locked beneath his hand. That same hand slowly lifted to push against the light switch, so that the room was illuminated only by the single shaded lamp beside the bed. Casey shook with a combination of desire and tension. The tension grew stronger when he made no further move to approach her.

"Undress for me, Casey."

Her body jerked at the bluntness of his demand. He appeared as unfeeling and cold as a statue, but she knew the image was false. She was being tested; he still retained a shred of control. He was giving her a chance to retreat, and in so doing, was making her take the final, irrevocable step in their relationship.

For just a moment she felt a resurgence of the old, debilitating sense of inadequacy Hugh had always aroused in her. But then she saw the fear in Chad's eyes; fear that she would wake in the morning hating him for his mastery of her body; fear that she would recoil from him in resentment, that she would once again spurn the love he had for her.

As though in a daze she began to unfasten the knot at her waist, her eyes eloquent with pride. She heard him gasp as the robe slipped from her shoulders. She knew her body was outlined by the light behind her, but she was no longer critical of its faults. She was reassured by the heat of Chad's slowly wandering blue eyes. She felt beautiful when she saw the awed expression of love on his strong, ruggedly masculine face. She reached out to him with a natural grace free from all self-consciousness, and he moved into her arms with an answering groan.

"Be very sure, Katherine," he whispered, his voice a tortured rasp against the sensitive flesh of her ear. "Because once I take you I'll never be able to let you go. I'll bind you to me forever."

"Without you forever is a long, lonely time, Chad." She drew back slightly, searching his face with a solemnity she found reflected in his eyes.

"Until now it *has* been long, and damnably lonely," he admitted.

Her face cupped in his hands, his fingers moved tenderly against her temples. "There have been women in my life, Katherine," he admitted, his mouth lifting with wry emphasis, "but when an affair ended I never looked back. I didn't think I'd ever find myself needing a woman so much that to be apart from her was a form of torture."

Her face crumpled, and she buried her head against his chest. "You don't know how much I want to be that woman for you."

His chest rose sharply and his arms tightened. "You are everything to me, sweetheart. From the instant I saw you through the crowd on that ship, I knew I'd found what I'd unconsciously been searching for all my life. I need your loving warmth to give me ease and your courage to give me strength."

Casey's hands clutched at the back of his robe, but she kept her face hidden from his gaze as she said, "When I told you I was very much a coward it was true, Chad. I'd hidden from my own needs for so long it had become a habit to ignore them. Then you came along, and I saw my feelings for you as a weakness. But something happened today that made me realize how wrong I've been to push love aside as though it held no place in my life."

Once again she lifted her eyes to his face, and

they shone with conviction as she whispered, "Today Sharon made me realize that only people can destroy love, Chad. At first what she said only made me feel shame at the way I've treated you. That's why I was so defensive with you tonight."

"And now?" he asked, his body tensing.

Slowly she lifted her arms until they circled his neck. "Now I know that love has given me strength, not taken it away, my darling." Her fingers cradled his head and pressed against his scalp until his mouth was merely a kiss away. "With your arms around me," she murmured, "I can face life with more courage than I've ever had before."

His lips sealed her promise with the heat of a passion no longer denied. The kiss blended need with tenderness, strength with vulnerability, and at last freed them both to express the fullness of their love for each other. With a choked cry Chad lifted her and carried her to his bed. His robe discarded, he leaned over her and searched her eyes. They were clear and bright, with no trace of uncertainty, no shadow to mar the happiness that shone from them.

"I want it all," he insisted, with an arrogance that made her smile. "I want a home with you and Jonathan, and a 'till death do us part' marriage."

Her smile widened with unfeigned delight. "Yes, darling."

He buried his mouth against her throat. "You won't be too proud to accept my help with the children while you work?"

He was sliding his body slowly downward, and

his tongue began to taste her breasts as she gasped, "Children?"

She felt his tongue curve around her hardening nipple. "Mmmm," he murmured, his lips nibbling hungrily. "We should provide a few playmates for our son, don't you think?"

Her voice resonated with delight in their future. "Oh, yes!"

It was then it began, the enchantment that kept them enthralled. In Chad's arms, Casey became the sea witch he had called her on the night they met. Higher and higher they rode the crest of the wave, their bodies shuddering together on a sea of desire. Again and again they came together as one being, one soul, and by morning both welcomed the dawning of the first day of their life together.

YOU'LL BE SWEPT AWAY WITH SILHOUETTE DESIRE

$1.95 each

11 ☐ James	37 ☐ James	63 ☐ Dee	89 ☐ Ross
12 ☐ Palmer	38 ☐ Douglass	64 ☐ Milan	90 ☐ Roszel
13 ☐ Wallace	39 ☐ Monet	65 ☐ Allison	91 ☐ Browning
14 ☐ Valley	40 ☐ Mallory	66 ☐ Langtry	92 ☐ Carey
15 ☐ Vernon	41 ☐ St. Claire	67 ☐ James	93 ☐ Berk
16 ☐ Major	42 ☐ Stewart	68 ☐ Browning	94 ☐ Robbins
17 ☐ Simms	43 ☐ Simms	69 ☐ Carey	95 ☐ Summers
18 ☐ Ross	44 ☐ West	70 ☐ Victor	96 ☐ Milan
19 ☐ James	45 ☐ Clay	71 ☐ Joyce	97 ☐ James
20 ☐ Allison	46 ☐ Chance	72 ☐ Hart	98 ☐ Joyce
21 ☐ Baker	47 ☐ Michelle	73 ☐ St. Clair	99 ☐ Major
22 ☐ Durant	48 ☐ Powers	74 ☐ Douglass	100 ☐ Howard
23 ☐ Sunshine	49 ☐ James	75 ☐ McKenna	101 ☐ Morgan
24 ☐ Baxter	50 ☐ Palmer	76 ☐ Michelle	102 ☐ Palmer
25 ☐ James	51 ☐ Lind	77 ☐ Lowell	103 ☐ James
26 ☐ Palmer	52 ☐ Morgan	78 ☐ Barber	104 ☐ Chase
27 ☐ Conrad	53 ☐ Joyce	79 ☐ Simms	105 ☐ Blair
28 ☐ Lovan	54 ☐ Fulford	80 ☐ Palmer	106 ☐ Michelle
29 ☐ Michelle	55 ☐ James	81 ☐ Kennedy	107 ☐ Chance
30 ☐ Lind	56 ☐ Douglass	82 ☐ Clay	108 ☐ Gladstone
31 ☐ James	57 ☐ Michelle	83 ☐ Chance	109 ☐ Simms
32 ☐ Clay	58 ☐ Mallory	84 ☐ Powers	110 ☐ Palmer
33 ☐ Powers	59 ☐ Powers	85 ☐ James	111 ☐ Browning
34 ☐ Milan	60 ☐ Dennis	86 ☐ Malek	112 ☐ Nicole
35 ☐ Major	61 ☐ Simms	87 ☐ Michelle	113 ☐ Cresswell
36 ☐ Summers	62 ☐ Monet	88 ☐ Trevor	114 ☐ Ross

Silhouette Desire

$1.95 each

115 ☐ James	134 ☐ McKenna	153 ☐ Milan	172 ☐ Stuart
116 ☐ Joyce	135 ☐ Charlton	154 ☐ Berk	173 ☐ Lee
117 ☐ Powers	136 ☐ Martel	155 ☐ Ross	174 ☐ Caimi
118 ☐ Milan	137 ☐ Ross	156 ☐ Corbett	175 ☐ Palmer
119 ☐ John	138 ☐ Chase	157 ☐ Palmer	176 ☐ Carey
120 ☐ Clay	139 ☐ St. Claire	158 ☐ Cameron	177 ☐ Monet
121 ☐ Browning	140 ☐ Joyce	159 ☐ St. George	178 ☐ Merrit
122 ☐ Trent	141 ☐ Morgan	160 ☐ McIntyre	179 ☐ Gordon
123 ☐ Paige	142 ☐ Nicole	161 ☐ Nicole	180 ☐ Berk
124 ☐ St. George	143 ☐ Allison	162 ☐ Horton	
125 ☐ Caimi	144 ☐ Evans	163 ☐ James	
126 ☐ Carey	145 ☐ James	164 ☐ Gordon	
127 ☐ James	146 ☐ Knight	165 ☐ McKenna	
128 ☐ Michelle	147 ☐ Scott	166 ☐ Fitzgerald	
129 ☐ Bishop	148 ☐ Powers	167 ☐ Evans	
130 ☐ Blair	149 ☐ Galt	168 ☐ Joyce	
131 ☐ Larson	150 ☐ Simms	169 ☐ Browning	
132 ☐ McCoy	151 ☐ Major	170 ☐ Michelle	
133 ☐ Monet	152 ☐ Michelle	171 ☐ Ross	

SILHOUETTE DESIRE, Department SD/6
1230 Avenue of the Americas
New York, NY 10020

Please send me the books I have checked above. I am enclosing $_____
(please add 75¢ to cover postage and handling. NYS and NYC residents please
add appropriate sales tax). Send check or money order—no cash or C.O.D.'s
please. Allow six weeks for delivery.

NAME_____

ADDRESS_____

CITY_____ STATE/ZIP_____

Silhouette Desire

Fall in love again for the first time every time you read a Silhouette Romance novel.

Take 4 books free—no strings attached.

Step into the world of Silhouette Romance, and experience love as thrilling as you always knew it could be. In each enchanting 192-page novel, you'll travel with lighthearted young heroines to lush, exotic lands where love and tender romance wait to carry you away.

Get 6 books each month before they are available anywhere else! Act now and we'll send you four touching Silhouette Romance novels. They're our gift to introduce you to our convenient home subscription service. Every month, we'll send you six new Silhouette Romance books. Look them over for 15 days. If you keep them, pay just $11.70 for all six. Or return them at no charge.

We'll mail your books to you *two full months before they are available anywhere else.* Plus, with every shipment, you'll receive the Silhouette Books Newsletter absolutely free. *And Silhouette Romance is delivered free.*

Mail the coupon today to get your four free books—and more romance than you ever bargained for.

Silhouette Romance is a service mark and a registered trademark of Simon & Schuster, Inc.